In Strange Worlds

Brenda Cheers

BIRDCALL PUBLISHING AUSTRALIA

www.brendacheersbooks.com

Copyright © 2014 Brenda Cheers

First Edition

Author image Sargaison / Brisbane Headshots

Cover image © Tamara Dragovic / iStockphoto.com

ISBN-13: 978-0-9922907-9-5

I dedicate this book to my mother.
She has always encouraged me to write
and is my number one fan.

Also by Brenda Cheers:

In Times of Trouble

In Conversations with Strangers

In a House in Yemen

In a Time Where They Belong (Strange Worlds #2)

In Strange

Worlds

Brenda Cheers

PROLOGUE

During this journey north it has become my habit to find high places where I have clear views of the world below. I look for any signs of life — human life — but am constantly disappointed.

From the journal of Meg Atkins, May 2013.

CHAPTER ONE

Meg's consciousness returned slowly. First she became aware of her throat — dry and sore — and full bladder. Her limbs were heavy, as though she'd been lying in the same position for too long. She couldn't hear anything — not a sound.

As she moved sideways to turn over, a searing pain hit her lower abdomen. Her eyes opened wide and she began panting, trying to breathe through the agony. Eventually the pain subsided to a dull ache.

The hospital ward was unfamiliar — not the one she'd been in when she'd first arrived. This one seemed more functional — less decorative. She scanned the room for any sign of baby equipment, but there wasn't any. Raising the bedclothes, she lifted her hospital gown and looked down at the dressing that was stuck firmly in a horizontal line across the top of her pubic bone. Clearly she'd had a caesarean section.

The situation with her bladder was becoming urgent. She manoeuvred to reach for the call button and pressed it long and hard. She heard it buzzing in a nearby nurses' station. Strangely, that was the only sound she could hear.

There was a drip stand by her bed. It held two bags which were sucked so dry they were compressed by vacuum. She looked further and found a full urine bag attached to the left side of the bed. She cursed the nursing staff and pressed the buzzer again. Where in the hell was everybody?

"Hello? Hello? Anybody there?" Her voice echoed through the corridors.

"Help! Help!" No response.

There was a telephone on the stand next to her bed. She had to move her body slightly to reach it, and the pain caused the room to darken and spin. She waited for this to pass before lifting the receiver and pressing zero for an outside line. If she called the hospital reception, she could tell them that something was wrong in her ward and she needed help. She dialled the number for directory information, and was surprised to find there was no answer.

She pressed the buzzer five times in quick succession. She called out louder. No response.

A piece of paper on the bedside table contained information about the hospital. It was printed on official stationery and had the telephone numbers at the bottom. Her shaking hand dialled the number. As the phone rang, she thought about what she was going to say. There was no answer.

"Think. Think." She lay back on the pillow and considered her situation.

How long had she been here? What exactly had happened?

She was scheduled for a caesarean section on the Monday —the specialist considering a natural birth unsafe after the two previous caesareans —but her waters had broken on the Thursday before that, and she'd moved quickly through the stages of labour. By the time the ambulance delivered her to the hospital, the contractions were coming so fast that the decision was made to allow the birth to proceed naturally.

She remembered the resident doctor being calm and controlling to begin with, issuing commands to the nurses in a low, level voice. This changed within a short time and she remembered the perspiration dripping from his forehead, the pitch of his voice rising, the blood on his hands —

Someone had grabbed her left hand and inserted a

needle. She had tried to talk, to ask what was happening, but the world went black.

She reached for the telephone again and dialled her mother's number. No answer. She wished she had her watch. There was light behind the curtains and it seemed bright, like early morning. She rang the number of a co-worker but it diverted to voicemail after several rings.

There was only one thing to do. Get out of the bed and see what was going on. How was she going to do that?

The drip bags were connected to a line in the back of her hand. Wincing, she removed the tape that held it in place, and then slowly extracted the needle.

She reached under the bedclothes and felt for the catheter line. Holding it firmly she gave it a tug, but it wouldn't move. How was it being held in? She tried again. It held stubbornly. She untied the bag from the side railing of the bed, and held it to her chest.

She knew from past caesareans that swinging her legs out of the bed was going to be painful. She did it as slowly as possible and felt for the floor with her toes, a task made difficult by her short legs. She stood, wobbling for a few seconds.

The door was only a few metres away, but by the time she got to it, she felt like she'd completed a marathon.

The door frame provided support as she looked out.

An orderly was lying on the floor of the corridor, sideways. She couldn't see his face, so she moved tiny step by tiny step until she could lean on the wall on the other side of the hallway. From there she could see him fully. The staring eyes, strange skin colour, and bloody mucous that was dried around his mouth, told her he was well and truly dead.

"Oh my God. Oh my God."

She had never seen a corpse before, and the sight of this one made the scene before her spin. She slid along the wall, scared that if she let go she'd faint.

She got to the nurses' station and peered over the counter top. There were two nurses, one male and one female, both with heads collapsed onto keyboards. Staring eyes and bloody lips told Meg all she needed to know. Bile rose in her throat and she spat into a kidney dish.

She knew now why everything was so quiet in the hospital. She began breathing in and out quickly, panic rising. Her only thoughts were to find her baby and get out of there.

First she had to get rid of the catheter. She shuffled to a spare computer terminal and opened a browser. Her search words were, "removing catheter". She read the results grimly, wondering how she could perform the Foley catheter removal procedure by herself. A mirror, a syringe, a steady hand. Despite trembling and sweating, she soon had it removed. Emptying her bladder was another problem, but she already knew the drill — run some water and be patient.

The relief was enormous, and the release of the pressure also helped lessen the pain at the site of her operation. She was left with an ache which she found debilitating, however, so located some analgesics and swallowed two.

The nursery was at the end of a corridor which had many wards running its length. As she passed each ward, she looked in, hoping to see signs of life. The patients were lying motionless in their beds, while the staff were either lying sprawled on the floor, or in chairs, slumped sideways.

The nursery was silent. She rested her forehead on the glass and stared at the figures, motionless, which were firmly wrapped in their cocoons of blankets. Was one of them her child? Each bassinet had a name in large letters at the base. She searched quickly, but none said 'Atkins'. She didn't know if this was good or bad. Perhaps the baby had survived the birth and was still alive in the neo-natal intensive care.

Her chart. That would tell her. She shuffled back to her room, trying to avoid seeing any more bodies. The chart was hooked to the end of the bed. She saw "Meg Atkins" and a patient number across the top. It took some time to understand the medical terms, but eventually the meaning became clear. As she read the details, hot tears fell onto the much-used pages. Stillborn. That was that then. She had to get out of there.

Hospital gowns aren't designed to be worn outside, and certainly not in Melbourne during May, but there had been no sign of her clothes, and she was desperate to leave the hospital. Whatever disease was spreading in there was something she didn't want to catch.

A cab to her house was the best plan. She could pay the driver with money from her emergency tin in the pantry.

The front doors of the hospital led to a car-park where nothing moved. She saw a SUV with the door ajar, and shuffled toward it. The driver was slumped over the wheel and as she opened the car door, his arm fell sideways. She looked over toward the road, expecting to see traffic, but nothing moved. She closed her eyes and listened. She heard a dog barking and a bird call. No traffic, no planes, no sounds of human life.

Luckily the driver of the SUV had slumped to his right, making it easy for her to pull him onto the ground. She stepped over his body to access the driver's seat, and was relieved to find the automatic transmission controls — a clutch would have been too difficult. It took some time to swing her legs in and reposition the seat. The clock said 6.45 a.m. Melbourne should have been waking up. She turned on the radio and searched around the stations, bracing for the voices of morning disc jockeys. The only sound she heard was static.

The SUV was full-featured, and she was able to set the GPS to take her home. In the streets she found cars that had come to complete stops, but seemingly without violence. In most cases she could see the drivers, slumped over the steering-wheels or leaning against the doors, all with the tell-tale bloody stains around their mouths. There were bodies on the footpaths, but not many. It seemed that whatever happened to everyone occurred in the late night or early morning when traffic was light and pedestrians were few.

Her house stood bathed in sunlight, its solid presence a comfort. She left the SUV on the street and walked up the driveway, puffing with exertion. The spare key was under the ficus pot, and she retrieved it with shaking hands. Suddenly she had to sit, and half fell onto the bench-seat on the front veranda.

The wood wasn't comfortable, but she was glad to rest for a few minutes and think.

Clearly it wasn't just the hospital that had suffered

this — what? Virus? Something had happened to the people of Melbourne. Without radio stations it was hard to find out what. The internet would tell her within seconds. She took a deep breath and got to her feet.

The key turned easily in the lock. She moved into the dim hallway, taking her cashmere coat from the rack as she did so. She slid her arms into the sleeves and was immediately cocooned in warmth.

From the kitchen she noticed that the deck was bathed in sunshine, so she undocked her tablet and walked through the French doors. Here she could sit in a comfortable seat and find out what the hell was going on.

None of the many news sites she visited had been updated since around one o'clock in the morning. She began by accessing the Australian sites but quickly became frustrated with this. The world news pages were no different. The enormity of what this meant began to overwhelm her and the slight tremor of her hands worsened to shaking. Afraid this would cause her to drop the tablet, she placed it on the table.

Her parents lived away from the city, in a small Gippsland town. Dialling the number again, she hoped her mother would pick up this time. Prayed that she would. No answer.

What about her ex-husband then? She tried Richards's mobile first, then his work number, quickly followed by the home number. She braced herself for a conversation with Lucy, but there was no answer.

The dawning horror of what this probably meant made Meg cry out loud. "No! No!" She rose unsteadily and wrapped the coat more tightly around herself.

The car she'd taken from the hospital was more comfortable than her own, so she climbed back into the driver's seat. The journey to Richard's house normally took around forty-five minutes, but with the streets empty it only took twenty. As she pulled into the street where she used to live, she noted the lack of activity on what would normally be a busy morning. This was a suburb created for the wealthy, and usually there would be SUV's, mostly black and with tinted windows, driving up and down its length. Nothing moved.

The front door was locked. She moved around to the back and tried all the doors and windows. Eventually she threw a rock through a glass door at the back, and unlatched it from the inside. An alarm began wailing. She went to the controls and entered a code, but Richard had obviously changed it since she'd lived there.

She passed the master bedroom, not bothering to

look inside. She was focused on the two doors further down the hallway.

The first of these doors had "Emily" in pink, wooden letters spread across the white surface. She leaned her head against the door and took a deep breath, turning the handle as she did so.

The room was bathed in yellow, which glowed from the walls ("Saffron" was the paint colour, she recalled) and the curtains that were white with a yellow check. Golden hair was spread across the pillow. Emily was facing the wall and Meg lowered herself down until she was lying on top of the bedclothes, spooned into Emily's back.

"Hello, fairy princess." Meg paused as though waiting for a response. She stroked Emily's hair.

"I suppose you want me to sing you the lullaby — you know — the one we made up that night when you couldn't sleep. Do you want me to sing it?" She paused again and cleared her throat.

"Sleep, sleep,
I need my sleep.
My eyelids are heavy,
I need to count sheep.
Sleep, sleep,
I need my sleep.

Come to me Teddy,

Let's breathe nice and deep.

Sleep, sleep...."

Meg stopped singing and wiped her eyes. "We didn't get to say goodbye. We always said proper goodbyes, remember? Once you were angry with me and tried to get away without giving me a kiss and cuddle, but you couldn't do that. You came running out before I drove off, just to say bye-bye properly." Meg smiled at the memory.

"This time we couldn't say a proper goodbye, but it's nobody's fault. It just happened that way. I hope you're not upset at that. I hope you understand..." Meg noticed a knot in Emily's hair and untangled it.

"I've come to say goodbye now — a bit late but I think it still counts. Hopefully you'll know — know that I've come to say a proper goodbye." Her breath was coming in shudders.

"You've always been my special fairy princess. We had such fun times together, remember? I used to take you to kindy and then not want to leave? We'd go early so I could play lots of puzzles with you and read books. You'd lean back against me and listen. You always wanted me to read each book twice." She took a deep breath and looked up at the ceiling.

"It's like that now. I want to pick up one of your books and read to you — just read and read and never stop. I don't want to leave you. It's too hard. There's a big empty spot just here." She pointed to a place under her heart. "It's empty without you. I want to be with you. I'm lonely and scared. So scared."

Meg lay silently for a long time. Eventually she rose with an exhalation of breath and kissed the top of Emily's head. She scanned the room until she found what she was looking for. It was the floppy bunny with the soft ears. She held it to her chest and walked to the door. As she looked back she had an impulse which made her move back to the bed and straighten the bedclothes until they were without creases. Then she left.

The second door was decorated with a skull and crossbones. This brought a half-smile to Meg's lips, but it quickly disappeared. She turned the handle but the door wouldn't budge. She considered forcing the door, but knew she didn't have the strength. Knowing Nicholas, he'd have a chair propped up under the door handle, just in case someone got through the locks.

She held her palm flat against the door for a moment and pictured how he would look. The bed-clothes would be twisted around his ankles, and his pyjamas, which always seemed to be too short in the legs, would be barely covering him. She wiped her eyes and moved back down the hallway.

Richard and Lucy were in a new king-sized bed. Richard was spooning into Lucy's back, and they looked peaceful. Meg, oddly, felt an emotion that was close to fondness rise in her. They did make a nice-looking couple.

She left through the front door, closing it firmly behind her. Should she make the two-hour drive to her parent's house? No, she had to go home and lie down. She had to find more pain killers. Above all else, she had to find answers.

Webcams were what eventually provided the answers for Meg. She found a site that provided links to live cameras in nearly thirty countries. She clicked on the "Times Square, New York" link. Although it was eight o'clock at night there, streetlights made it possible to see bodies lying in the street. Smoke drifted across the camera lens in clouds. She moved to Germany — Hamburg. Not a live person to be seen, only fires and motionless peak-hour traffic which blocked all freeways. It was clearly more chaotic in the northern hemisphere where everyone had died during the daytime. If you were a survivor there, it would be far worse than it was for Meg.

She was in her office, using the desktop computer and dual monitors that worked more efficiently than the tablet. Oddly, her office chair was comfortable and it had the added advantage of wheels that rolled well on the timber flooring. With minimal effort she could move between rooms, using her arms on the walls to propel herself.

The webcams were addictive. She visited Africa, North America, South America, Europe and Asia. She could see fires burning in almost every northern hemisphere location and wondered about them. She found a camera in New Zealand that showed Auckland's skyline. No large fires there. What she didn't find on any webcam site was evidence of human life. On impulse she searched for and found a webcam in the Antarctic settlement of Mawson Station. It seemed to be just a static shot taken at midday on the day before.

Her searches became faster and wilder as her fingers raced from key to key. Finally she turned the chair away from the desk and covered her face with trembling hands. "Oh my God. Oh my God." Panic was rising; it hit her stomach, chest and throat. She breathed deeply and counted each exhalation.

In an attempt to calm herself, she tried to work out a puzzle. Why were there so many fires in the northern hemisphere? The answer came to her. It had been daytime there. People had been cooking meals, ironing clothes, refuelling vehicles, piloting aircraft and driving trains when they died. Some fires would have been triggered immediately, others would have taken longer.

She opened the mail client and sent a global message to every contact in her address book. Then she sent an SMS message to every person she knew. She went to Facebook and Twitter and left messages which asked anyone who saw her message to contact her. She opened a blog she'd used to record a holiday she and Richard had taken, and made a posting which read, "Is anyone there? I'm in Australia and am searching for anyone in the world who is alive." She added the tags: pandemic, global deaths, all people dead, holocaust.

There was one more person she wanted to check on. Sandy had been her best friend since school days. They had both gotten married and divorced. They'd drifted in and out of each other's lives depending on what was happening at the time, but were always available to the other in times of crisis.

As she drew up to Sandy's house she heard a dog howling. That would be Buster. She tried the front door and it opened, which was not unusual — Sandy was a bit lax on security. Buster jumped up and his paws hit her incision. She gasped and growled at him. He ran to the bedroom door and looked back at her.

A very bad smell became stronger the closer she got to the bedroom. She put her nose in the crook of her elbow, and kept moving forward.

Sandy wasn't alone. She was lying on her side facing the window and there were bloodstains on the pillow. The man was facing the other direction, his back to Meg, but she recognised the head. It was Craig, the bastard. How long had this been going on? And what sort of best friend was she?

The anger rose quickly but dissipated just as fast. She and Craig had broken up months ago — when Meg first told Craig she was pregnant with his child, the one she'd just been in hospital having. He wasn't Meg's man and Sandy hadn't really betrayed her. It just felt like she had.

Unless ... she had first introduced them not long before he broke up with her. Maybe they'd gotten together straight after that meeting and had been in a relationship since. What did it matter now though? There were more important things to consider.

The smell was coming from Craig and she figured he must have voided his bowels when he died. Seemed appropriate somehow, being sent to eternity lying in his own shit.

Buster had left through the open front door. Meg

called him but he didn't re-appear. She took a last look around Sandy's bohemian house — all bright colours and floating fabrics — and headed home.

Back at her desk, Meg opened the mail client and found that nobody had replied to her global email. No one had commented on her blog entry. The silence was deafening.

She swivelled in her seat and looked out the window into her garden. Birds were darting in and out of the bushes while making chirping noises. There were several dogs howling. The lack of human sound was almost deafening.

She couldn't be the only person left in the world. The idea in itself was a sort of a joke. How could she be? Why would she be?

The webcam site was still open and she moved from camera to camera, opening and closing the links quickly as each showed nothing but death.

Why would she alone survive? Was it something in her genetic make-up? Maybe it was the cocktail of drugs that she was being given since the caesarean that protected her.

A thought made her stop totally still. She had stopped the drugs — those that had been feeding into her through the drip. What if this meant she was no longer protected? Was she incubating some sort of virus? Was she going to die soon?

Terror rose in her, but it was replaced with a sort of acceptance. What would she want to live for anyway? She'd gone from having three children to none. She wasn't in a relationship. There was nobody to talk to, to share her life with. Even her best friend was dead. Her parents were probably dead.

Her boss, too. How sad. That incredible woman — intelligent, driven and caring. How could such a force of nature be dead so young? How could she have died while Meg lived? It just didn't seem right — didn't make sense. Meg wanted to hear Angela's voice one last time so dialled her mobile and waited until the call was diverted to voicemail. The message began and Meg listened, knowing it would be the last time she heard Angela's voice — low, businesslike. She didn't end the call until after the last word was spoken. By this time her sobs were causing the whole of her body to shake.

She put the mobile phone on the desk and wheeled herself into the bathroom. There was a set of hair clippers in the cupboard that she kept for Nicky's hair. They buzzed loudly as she lifted section after section of blonde curls and sheared them off, dropping each to the floor. She was sobbing and could hardly see herself in the mirror for the flow of tears. Then it was done. She levered herself up from the chair and looked closer at her reflection before moving to lean against the bathroom wall. Slowly she slid to the hair-strewn floor and arranged herself in a foetal position. She lay there sobbing until there were no tears left.

"You should get drunk," said a voice in Meg's head.

"No. That's a really bad idea."

"Why?"

"You know why. I go bad when I drink. Besides, I have no alcohol."

"Yes you have. Remember the vodka that Sandy left in your freezer?"

"Ah, vodka. Yeah. That's not too bad. I could drink it with cranberry juice or orange. Might not be a good idea with the painkiller I'm taking, though."

"What does it matter now? What does anything matter now?"

"Yeah, that's true."

"Good. Now you've got the idea. Let's do it."

She woke with a pounding head and terrible thirst. Her head was on the desktop and she had drooled over a pad of post-it notes. A stapler was resting under her forehead. The empty vodka bottle was on the floor next to a smashed glass.

Food wrappers were spread across the floor and she remembered the terrible alcohol-induced hunger attack that had hit her at some stage through the evening. She had raided the refrigerator and pantry for anything that didn't require preparation or cooking. It seemed she'd found quite a lot.

Her stomach began heaving. She covered her mouth and leapt from the chair without thinking. The pain forced her to the floor. She crawled to the bathroom and vomited then dry-retched for what felt like an eternity. The pain of the heaving was excruciating to the healing flesh. When she finished she crawled to her bedroom and slept the sleep of the dead.

Meg and Richard are standing in Montville, a small township in the Sunshine Coast hinterland in Queensland. They are gazing into the window of a real estate agent's office, and Meg is amused by the reflection displayed — Richard's tall frame compared to her own squat, solid one.

Richard is talking in his usual authoritative tone, telling Meg about the area and how it attracts those people looking for an alternative lifestyle.

"They have rainwater tanks and grow their own fruit and veggies. Suits those folk who have paranoia about what's being added to their food." Richard has no such qualms — eats anything with gusto.

"Their belief in self-sufficiency goes further than that. Many of them generate their own power from the sun, wind and in other ways."

Meg is looking around, noticing the difference between the holiday-makers and the local population. They are easy to tell apart. The locals look like they have sprung up from the soil — organic, sort of.

"I just can't get over how green and lush everything looks." She takes a breath of the clean air and smiles.

"That's 'cause of all the rain. This ridge has its own micro-climate." He points to the coast, which is a long way down. "The sea air rushes up this mountain range from down there. It cools really quickly and forms into rain. The precipitation isn't measured in millimetres here, but in metres. Pisses down constantly. Wouldn't suit you — your hair would be frizzy 24/7."

Meg laughs. "But it mustn't be just the rain. Look at how lush and healthy the bushes and trees are."

"That's the other thing — the soil. The joke is that you just have to shove anything in the ground and it grows overnight."

The village has a nice feel about it — just like a

country town.

Richard's grin is lopsided. "It would be a great place to come and live when the world finally fucks up."

Meg woke from the dream with Richard's words still echoing in her head. Did they ever have that conversation while holidaying on the Sunshine Coast?

They had rented a holiday apartment in Noosa and had spent one of the seven days exploring the hinterland, all along the ridge from Mapleton to Maleny. They had parked in Montville and walked in and out of quaint stores: art galleries, potter's sheds, clothing stores and even a shop that sold cuckoo clocks. They had enjoyed huge bowls of steaming soup in a cafe that had paintings of poets hung around its walls, and which boasted extraordinary views down to the coast.

This all happened in the early days, before becoming parents, when they still held hands and had long talks on all sorts of subjects. She couldn't recall them having the same conversation as she had just dreamed, though.

He was right about one thing, that Richard in the dream. With its high precipitation and magic soil, Montville was certainly a good place to go if your survival depended on producing your own food, water and power.

She was in the shower, removing the waterproof dressing from the wound. The scar was raised and red and she wondered about removing the stitches. When should she do that?

The dream had got her thinking about matters of survival, and as the warm water soothed her ravaged body she thought about the basics. Electricity was the big one. How much longer would it last? She guessed that it would depend how long a fault would take to develop. Once that happened the end of the power supply would be rapid.

How about town water? Was that dependent on the regular power supply? Was it pumped out of dams?

The internet. How long could that stay up once the servers around the world went down?

She reached for shampoo and squeezed a dollop into her hand before realising she had no hair to wash. She laughed without humour, and washed the product down the drain.

At least she felt better after her long sleep. The pain had lessened and some energy was returning. She longed for a walk through the local parks, the same way she used to go when the world was normal. It was a loop that would take forty-five minutes. In her present condition she figured she could do one park and it would take around a third of that time.

She stepped out from the shower and dried herself. The bathroom mirror was fogged but she could still see enough to make her want to cry. She was bald and had circles under her eyes. Her scar stood out like a heavily painted mouth. She thought she looked like a survivor from some terrible ordeal, then realised she was exactly that.

Her shorts and t-shirt were too thin for the cool day. She added a track top and slid into her running shoes without undoing the laces. At the front door she saw her grandmother's walking stick and decided to take it with her in case her legs became weak.

The walking stick had stood in that exact place by the front door for as long as Meg could remember. After her grandmother had passed away and left the house to Meg, the stick became one of her favourite objects, as it evoked images of that wonderful old woman. Meg had renovated the house in order to rent it to tenants, but as her marriage stumbled and broke, the house became her refuge and she could still remember the sense of satisfaction and rightness she felt as she placed the walking stick back where it belonged — by the front door.

The first part of the walk was uneventful, and it felt

good. That changed, however, when she saw a shape hurtling toward her from the left. It was a dog, lean and sinewy like a greyhound, and its teeth were bared. A growling sound came from its throat. It looked hungry.

It had brought Meg to a standstill and she considered her next move carefully. Never having owned a dog placed her in a position of disadvantage. Should she just stand still and hope it went on its way? Should she try to talk soothingly? Should she hit it with the walking stick?

She was startled from these thoughts by the arrival of another dog. It came bounding into the park and ran toward her in a straight line. The first dog turned and faced it. The two of them circled each other, snarling and growling. The newcomer pounced and they began rolling across the grass, trying to get at each other's throats.

Meg backed away slowly, breaking into a faster hobble as soon as she was out of sight of the dogs. She guessed that there would be many more hungry domestic pets roaming the streets and perhaps they would view her as food. What would happen to all the dogs and cats locked in houses with their owners? She had been hearing their mournful cries. They would starve. Would they eat their dead owners?

This thought, and the exertion and fear made her nauseous. She made a beeline for her house.

The end of electrical supply, when it came, arrived without warning. Meg was randomly surfing the internet when the monitors went black and the CPU stopped whirring. She checked the circuit board, hoping the safety switch had been tripped, but no such luck.

Her next hope, that the supply would be magically reinstated, was also in vain. She wandered aimlessly through the house, thinking about what this really meant, knowing that the city was no longer a place to live.

Five days had passed since she woke in the hospital. Five whole days that she'd let drift by without making any plans. She knew why. It was because she wasn't even sure she wanted to carry on. She had waited to see if she too would die with blood foaming out of her mouth. Then, when it seemed this wasn't going to happen, she had considered taking her own life.

It seemed to Meg, as she wandered through her much-loved house, that it was time to make a firm decision about her future and then take action. If she wasn't to die then she was to work hard at survival.

Focusing on any one thought had become difficult for her but she had to do it.

Where was she to go? Probably the Sunshine Coast

hinterland, just like in her dream.

How was she to get there? The only option was to drive.

What in? The nice SUV she took from the hospital? It didn't look like much of a workhorse. Perhaps she could visit a motor dealer. She realised then that she could just walk in and take her pick of any vehicle. Perhaps a four-wheel-drive. It would be rugged and roomy.

How long would it take to drive there? Two days of long driving.

What would she need? Clothing, toiletries, tablet and laptop. Food. A full tank of fuel. Damn, the service stations needed electricity to pump petrol. She'd cross that bridge when she came to it.

What else?

Protection against the ever increasing numbers of angry, hungry and confused dogs that had begun hunting in packs.

Tools to break into shops and service stations.

A method of getting fuel out of underground tanks.

She was well aware of the need for urgency and vowed to be ready to leave within twenty-four hours.

It took Meg half a day cruising around car dealerships and

used car lots to find the perfect vehicle, but it was worth it. A rugged, late model four-wheel-drive, used but with low mileage.

The previous owner had made some improvements that lifted her spirits: a refrigerator in the back, an extra heavy-duty battery; an extra spare wheel. She just needed the keys.

The showroom was modern and heavily secured. Her first attempts to gain entry were almost comic in their futility, and frustration rose quickly. Two objects thrown against the glass simply bounced back at her.

Finally she got back behind the wheel of the SUV and drove it to the showroom window. She had to mount a concrete ledge that ran around the building, but once over that she was able to touch the glass with the bumper bar. She accelerated slowly until the glass fell inward, smashing on the tiled floor.

After finding the keys in an office marked "Stock Control" she was at last able to unlock the four-wheel drive and inspect it. It was full-featured, with a sunroof and cruise control. It came equipped with GPS and long-range fuel tanks. Even better, these tanks were three-quarters full of fuel.

The interior was larger than Meg expected and for a

while it looked like she would have problems reaching the accelerator and brake pedals. The vehicle wasn't designed for short-legged drivers. After fiddling with the electronic seat controls, she finally achieved a drivable position, and decided that she had to have this vehicle.

To manoeuvre the four-wheel-drive out of its position on the lot was difficult. She had to move six other cars. At one stage she was so tired and frustrated by the process of having to match keys to the cars and then find a place to move each one to, that she felt like giving up. She walked back into the showroom and drank a glass of water. She swivelled in the used car manager's chair for a few minutes and drew sketches of the model cars that sat on his desk. Finally she was able to continue freeing the four-wheel-drive from its position.

Having this vehicle made the decision to leave Melbourne a bit easier, and she even considered leaving that evening. She had already packed what she needed to take, after all. What changed her mind was realising that the darkness might cloak hazards. She decided to wait until first light.

That night she wandered through her grandmother's house, wishing she could transport it to Queensland with her. She had never understood the wishes outlined in her Nana's will — why the house was left to her. The logical person to bequeath it to would have been Meg's father — her grandmother's son.

Did her grandmother see what Meg didn't, that her marriage was doomed to fail and that she'd need a home of her own? Or was it just that Nana saw that Meg loved the house. Or maybe she simply wanted to give her only grandchild something of value.

It was a warm and welcoming home, solidly built in the worker's-cottage style. Meg, as a child, had always slept soundly while visiting her grandmother in the school holidays. As an adult, she found the magic sleeping qualities still existed in the home. It was hard to leave.

In the fresh morning air, however, Meg was able to lock the door and walk purposefully to the four-wheel-drive without too much regret. She placed Emily's floppy-eared bunny in the passenger seat before starting the engine and driving away.

Her original plan was to drive north through Tullamarine and join onto the Hume Highway. This would eventually put her on the Newell Highway which was the quickest way to reach Queensland. It was inland driving all the way.

One thought made her change these plans — her

parents. Logic dictated that they had died with everybody else, but she couldn't be certain. What if the gene or whatever that saved her from dying was given to her by her mother or father? They too could have survived.

The fact that they hadn't been answering their telephone wasn't a good sign. They were never far from home and always easy to contact. The messages she had left on their answering machine had gone unanswered.

There were a few 'what-ifs' though. Her mother was listed as next-of-kin on the hospital admittance form. She would have been notified of Meg's condition. They may have been on their way to see her? What if her father was driving and crashed the car when he died but her mother survived. What if...?

There was only one thing to do — drive to her parent's house, taking the route she knew they'd take, but in reverse. She could look out for their car, and then check their house. She needed to do this before moving on.

It was an easy drive along the Princes Highway down to South-East Gippsland, made even easier by the absence of any other vehicles. There were some obstacles — large trucks that had come to grief when the drivers had died — and in some cases this caused her to divert, but the built in GPS always found a way for her.

She found her parents' green sedan in the carport attached to the house. She let herself in to their home through a side door that she had a key to. The stench that assaulted her made her back out quickly, but not before she'd seen their packed cases by the door. Clearly they had planned to be with her in the hospital, but were waiting for daylight to make the journey. They just never saw morning.

Her father's shed was an Aladdin's cave of things she needed. There was a .22 rifle hidden in a metal chest under the workbench. There were bolt-cutters and crowbars and mallets, all necessary for breaking into shops and other places. She found spare rounds for the rifle and a first aid kit.

She placed the rifle next to the driver's seat and kept the rounds in her pockets. Could she actually shoot dogs? She used to go rabbit hunting with her father and took her turn at shooting them. Would a dog be that much different, especially if it viewed you as its dinner? She thought not.

Before resuming the journey, she sat on the patch of buffalo grass at the front of her parent's house and closed her eyes for a moment. She pictured her mother the last time she saw her — that crease of worry hovering between her mother's eyebrows. During every conversation since Meg's marriage failure, her mother had questioned Meg relentlessly until satisfied that she wasn't in danger of a breakdown or self-harm.

Then she thought of her father, a hardworking man — generous and gregarious. Meg had many fond memories of him, and these ran through her mind: fishing trips, rabbit shooting, watching him shave, keeping him company in his tool shed when her mother was in a bad mood and wanted them both out from 'beneath her feet'. In her mother's eyes, she and her father always seemed to be partners in crime, a sentiment made stronger by their physical likenesses — both of them short and stocky. Her father would get a twinkle in his eye and say, "Let's face it, darling girl— we're both built like brick dunnies!" He would then fall about laughing.

A sense that something wasn't right made Meg open her eyes. Lined up along her parent's wire fence was a pack of dogs. Ten pairs of eyes watched her every move. Some had saliva dripping from their jaws. As she stood, one growled and flung itself against the wire. Others began doing the same and the air filled with barking and snarling.

That wasn't where her unease came from, however. It was from the air. People raised in the Australian bush learn to pay attention to what the atmosphere tells them. Meg could feel the wind gaining force. It was coming from the west in gusts and it felt like a hairdryer was being waved in her direction. This was unusual for autumn.

A flock of crows descended into the eucalyptus tree next to her and began cawing. At such close range the sound was terrible. She decided to begin driving again.

Reversing out, Meg twisted around and raised herself from the seat to view where the dogs were in relation to the wire gate. To open it would mean leaving the safety of the car, so, after a moment's consideration, she accelerated and ran the whole structure down. Some of the fence fell with it — the dogs having to move quickly to avoid being trapped underneath. She drove straight toward the pack, and they scattered. She could have run them down without compunction, such was her mood.

The loss of her parents, under normal circumstances, would have had a devastating effect on Meg, but coming as it did, after Nicholas, Emily, the stillborn child, Angela, and Sandy, the grief was numbed down. It felt like a safety switch had been flicked on in her brain to dull the emotions. She was still able to function.

Within a few minutes of leaving her parent's house she was back on the Princes Highway. Now she was certain there was nothing to keep her in the state of Victoria. Queensland it was, then.

CHAPTER TWO

Meg was a capable driver, but not a confident one. Richard had always been scathing of her ability, using his sarcasm at every turn until she refused to drive when he was a passenger.

By the time their marriage broke down, her confidence had been eroded to the point where she was nervous if she had to drive anywhere that was new to her. To now drive over two thousand kilometres alone was a major undertaking. Her mood was one of excited nervousness.

North of Traralgon, she began to see a smudge on the horizon and was unsure of its source— smoke or clouds. Small fires had been a feature of her journey to that point so she guessed the former. As she approached the township of Sale, she could see that smoke was indeed the cause, and it was heavy. The closer she came to Sale, the darker the skies became.

Then she could smell smoke. She closed the sunroof and windows and pressed the switch for the air-conditioning. The town of Sale came and went and she drove on, noticing that the sun had turned a blood-red. Bushfire? Surely not. Not at the end of May. Too late in the year.

She came to a bend in the Princes Highway and, as the road veered right, she saw a gully to the left. It was full of dark smoke and as she drew even, she saw a fireball the size of a car shooting out of the trees. When it hit the paddock of dry grass it exploded into flames. Meg swerved in shock and slowed her speed.

Then she could see the fire front — could see the flames leaping high into the sky. More fireballs came sailing her way, some flew over the car. Wherever they landed, a new fire would start.

Having grown up in South Gippsland, she knew about bushfires and had seen the devastation left behind. What she'd never done was drive so close to one. She knew it was very dangerous and that many had perished in her situation. What she also knew was that it was useless changing course or trying to outrun a large fire, as they changed direction suddenly, and would travel at speeds that a person could never imagine possible.

Her only chance was to stay calm and keep driving at

a reasonable speed — not too slow, not too fast. Both hands gripped the steering wheel, and her knuckles shone white.

There was no sky. The world was thick and black. Sometimes she could see the flames, and other times not. She would pass through areas already burned, and others that hadn't been touched.

She was only five years old when the "Ash Wednesday" fires had struck, but still remembered the photographs in the newspapers. One in particular remained firmly in her memory — three burned out cars on a road, no survivors.

More recent were the Black Saturday fires in 2009 which resulted in 173 deaths, many of the victims having expired in their vehicles. Meg's mouth was a thin line across a pale face as fires danced and trees exploded around her.

Kilometre after kilometre she travelled with the knowledge that her life was in peril, but as she approached Bairnsdale the sky lightened. She stomped on the accelerator and sped through the town, and didn't relax until thirty-five kilometres later when she arrived at Lakes Entrance. Here, surrounded by lakes on one side and Bass Strait on the other, she felt safe.

The strongest emotion Meg experienced after driving through the firestorm, was the need to tell somebody about it, or turn to a companion and say, "Gee, that was close!" and watch them roll their eyes in relief, or hear them suggest a beer to wash the smoke away.

Her only companion was Emily's floppy bunny and he wasn't saying much.

The need to communicate was almost overwhelming, and after giving the problem some thought, she broke into a stationer's and searched the shelves for writing tools. Eventually she emerged with a fountain pen, two boxes of cartridges and a journal bound in leather.

After stowing her gear at a Motor-Inn opposite the waterfront, Meg walked across the road and sat at a small marina and filled her lungs with the fresh air. For a few minutes she watched the bobbing of small boats and listened to the cries of gulls. Then she opened the fresh journal.

"This is day nine of being on my own and I guess this is a diary or a journal or something. I've never really had a journal. I don't think I'm much of a writer but I think it would be good for me to put my thoughts on paper, because I haven't got anyone to talk to.

On May 13th 2013 I woke up but it seems that no one else did. Now I'm an orphan and a mother who has lost three children, one during childbirth and two through whatever killed everyone.

And what was that? What could possibly kill every human being in the world at the same time? Well, not every human being. There's still me but I get scared when I think about that. I don't think about it often.

I'm used to being able to get on the internet and find the answer to anything. But there was no one alive to report what killed everyone! How stupid is that? So I don't know.

I'm on my way to Montville or Maleny to find somewhere to live. Somewhere to survive.

Today I drove through a bushfire. It seemed — well — like it was trying to get at me. Sinister, if that's the right word. With all that hell around me I felt like I was caught in the middle of a fight between good and evil. Somehow the good side won and I survived.

I wanted to talk about it — when I was safe, but now I find I'm too tried and emotional.

That's enough now. More later."

Refuelling the four-wheel-drive didn't end up being a problem for Meg. Some towns had lost electricity, but others hadn't and it was in these places that she would refill the tanks and jerry cans.

She always opted for the larger 24-hour stations that hadn't switched off the pumps on the night everyone died.

Otherwise she'd have to break into the shop and find the power switch.

In the towns that still had electricity, the traffic lights would still be working. If there was a clear view of the intersecting street, she would ignore the lights. If not, she would stop at a red light, her logic being that there might be one other survivor, and they might be driving in the opposite direction and how sad would it be if both of them were wiped out in a traffic accident?

It took her several hours to realise she didn't really need her seatbelt anymore. It took another day after that to lose the habit of automatically clicking the buckle into place. She loved driving on toll roads, knowing she'd never have to pay the charges. She began speeding, opening the sunroof and enjoying the fresh air. In one town she found some old blues CD's and played them loudly as the coastline sped past.

"I feel free. I could spend all day naked if I wished (I don't) and I don't have to worry about make-up or hair. Just now everything is good because I can just get food from shops and eat when I'm hungry. I usually stock up in towns where there is still electricity so I don't have to put up with the smell of rotting food. My diet isn't the best right now — I've been eating mostly convenience food — but I'll fix that when I'm settled on the Sunshine Coast.

Yesterday I saw a pretty beach and drove there on impulse.

The water was cold, but I stripped off and dived in. It took my breath away but it was fantastic."

She was constantly watching for signs to lookouts. It became her habit to drive to these, often up steep winding roads until she had a view of the world around her. She would scan the panorama, looking intently at each feature, searching for signs of human life. Eventually she would walk slowly back to the vehicle, her shoulders drooping, and drive to the next one.

As she passed through Batemans Bay, on the coast of New South Wales, Meg felt a pang of nostalgia. Her parents had brought her here on a holiday once when she was a pre-teen and although she didn't remember much about the trip, just the name of the town made her stomach clench in grief.

She circled the outskirts for a few minutes and then sat in a park overlooking the broad Clyde River while eating some potato snacks. Seagulls came to snatch crumbs, and as she finished the packet, she scattered the remains across the grass.

A growling from behind made her realise she'd acted stupidly. The rifle was in the four-wheel-drive which was parked twenty metres or so away. She stood slowly and walked away, not turning to meet the gaze of the dogs. Time slowed, each second seeming to last for minutes until she was safely behind the steering wheel, which she clutched tightly. There were around fifteen dogs, their ribs standing out like fingers on a clenched hand. Should she shoot them? No, the aggression she had felt towards dogs while at her parent's house had lessened and she didn't have the stomach for it.

Instead, she turned the key in the ignition and let the GPS guide her back on to the main road.

As she crossed the Brisbane River, an impulse made her drive through the western suburbs and up on to Mount Coot-tha. From there she had a broad view to the islands in Moreton Bay as well as the city of Brisbane which was rising out of the misty morning.

The river was like a fat brown snake, twisting and turning on its journey to the bay. It looked peaceful, but this could be deceptive. Just like a snake it could turn suddenly and cause chaos and heartbreak as in the floods of 2011.

Meg closed her eyes and listened, the same as she did at the top of every lookout she'd ascended. Dogs, birds, wind, leaves rustling, a piece of paper being blown across concrete — no man-made sounds.

As she stretched and rotated her spine, she saw smoke spiralling into the air from one of the islands and was reminded of the bushfire. She then thought about the chaos she'd seen on the webcams in the Northern Hemisphere and compared that to the view before her. That led to a thought about nuclear reactors used in power stations and she considered the problem of no one monitoring them. At least there were none in Australia as far as she knew.

The GPS told her she'd be in Montville in around one and a half hours. All of a sudden she was impatient to get there.

CHAPTER THREE

As Meg sped up the mountain to Maleny, she recalled the last time she'd travelled up to the top of the range. Richard had been driving, and was swearing under his breath at trucks that were labouring up the steep inclines. He'd take risks to get past one, only to find himself behind another. He always seemed to take such things personally. Richard didn't like anything in his way.

The four-wheel-drive didn't falter while ascending the steep incline; it just dropped some gears and kept up the momentum. It was she who decided to slow, and that was because of the vista that had just opened before her. Meg remembered the region as being beautiful, but the reality far exceeded the memory.

The view to the right, which took in the Sunshine Coast, was magnificent in its scale. Meg could see the entire stretch of coastline, the view made soft and blue by what she guessed was salt-spray. To the left were the rolling hills, and they were dotted with trees — many of them rounded at the top. There were no harsh angles to be seen — everything was curved and soft. The colours were extraordinary.

This was why she was driving at almost walking speed when she saw the tourist sign which indicated a resort down a side road. A travel magazine had featured the place, which was built along Obi-Obi Creek, and she had marvelled at the well-appointed cabins that were spread over a grassed area. She remembered how, in the accompanying images, the cabins resembled dice scattered over a gambling table.

And there it was. She parked and opened the door, allowing her legs a few seconds to stretch before dropping to the ground. She could see the reception area and a path alongside. Remembering to take the rifle, she went to explore.

Cabin six seemed to have the best situation, but when she peered inside, she could see that it had been occupied on the night of May 13. Cabin five was empty, but when she tried the door-handle it resisted. Rather than force her way in, she went back to reception and broke into the office. A quick search found the keys in an unlocked drawer. Before she left the office she crossed her fingers and flicked a switch. The resulting glow of the light bulb put a smile on her face.

Opposite reception was a restaurant which she glanced into. Linen tablecloths, gleaming cutlery and shining glassware — all high quality.

It was the cabin she was most interested in, and when she opened the door and smelled the freshness of the interior, she knew she'd come to the right place. It boasted an enclosed fireplace with glass door, a huge shower recess with two shower heads, a timber spa-bath, air-conditioning, fluffy robes and slippers, and best of all; a king bed with crisp, white sheets. It even had a kitchenette with microwave oven.

The only wash she'd had on the entire road trip was her brief swim in the ocean. Excitedly, she threw off her clothes and let the hot water of the shower soothe her travel-weary limbs.

The cabin door was still open, so she closed it in case of hungry dogs. She walked into the bedroom and within minutes was between the sheets and deeply asleep.

In the restaurant she made a decision to throw out any of the food that might have had its freshness compromised by power outages or time that had elapsed.

She found a garbage bag and threw most of the contents of the refrigerators into it. Fish, beef, chicken, pork and duck were all sacrificed. She decided the eggs could stay, as well as some salmon which had been sealed by cryovac and had a use by date in the future.

Some tomatoes were still passable and the parmesan cheese looked as though she could take a chance on it. Soon she had a delicious omelette on a plate. She wished she had some fresh bread to go with it.

There were some pieces of fruit in a bowl that she juiced and, as she surveyed her feast, she felt something close to contentment.

"I'm really happy at this resort. I know it's temporary — I need to move on and find a place that generates its own power and has a water supply, but for the time being I feel very good here.

After my long sleep I woke with a picture in my mind of what my new home will be, and the words 'rammed-earth' came to mind. The block it's built on will be several acres in size and the house will sit on it as if it sprouted from the soil. It will be a single-story dwelling with verandas all the way around.

Today I will rest and explore the village of Maleny. Tomorrow I will begin the search for my new home.

Although I feel moments of happiness, they are fleeting. Soon I am plunged back into thoughts of all the loved ones I've lost. I think 'why me?' and sometimes this takes me to a dark place where my sanity is threatened. I must stay away from that place. I must make the choice to be positive, somehow.

My subconscious wants me to be positive. It sends me thoughts. While I was waking from that long sleep in the gorgeous bed, I was remembering what Angela, my boss, told me once. It was after she'd seen the results of my psychometric test and called me in for an interview. She told me she'd never once seen this test fail in all the years she'd been using it, and she used it on hundreds of people a year. "Your results show you are capable of quick improvisation. You are innovative and intuitive." My face must've registered disbelief and she laughed. "No, it's true. Let me guess, you're just out of a bad relationship, are you?" I nodded. "Your man was a bit of a bastard — hurt your self-esteem?" I felt tears forming. "It's okay honey. I see it all the time. Believe me when I say that someday you'll look back on this part of your life and laugh. But this," she tapped the report. "This doesn't lie. You have exactly the same profile as several of my best-ever P.A's. That's why I've called you in here. I need you."

Angela was there for me from day one, boosting my self-image, buying me a gym membership, giving me vouchers for beauty treatments. She sent me to a wardrobe consultant who showed me what style of clothing to wear to suit my unusual build. When I saw the results in the mirror, I could hardly believe my eyes. Longer legs, smaller bum, well-proportioned chest — I looked normal!

Within six months I was better than I'd been at any stage of my life. I was rewarded one day when I collected Nicholas and Emily from Richard's house. I normally had to deal with Jodie, but this time Richard was home and came out to ask me a question. He stopped in his tracks and looked me up and down. I saw his eyebrows rise and a lazy smile come to his lips. I knew that expression — it was one he had always used on other women. Attractive women. Do you know how good that made me feel?

The psychometric test was right — I was a brilliant P.A. My job often required me to achieve the impossible for Angela and I always pulled through for her. I could pull rabbits out of hats like nobody else. Gee, I miss Angela — probably more than any other adult person I can think of.

So I woke from my deep sleep with Angela's words in my head, reminding me that I'm special and can cope with situations that would normally throw other people out of kilter. It reminded me that I have a particular hard-wiring in my brain that will help me survive in this new world. I think I'm going to need it."

Meg's days fell into a pattern. On waking she would check all the social media sites, emails and blogs, her disappointment at not finding any replies diluted by not really expecting any after all this time.

A walk around the perimeter of the resort would come next, and she took comfort from feeling her strength returning. She enjoyed hearing her feet thud as she stepped across a small bridge that spanned a creek. Dogs didn't seem to be a problem in this region and she wondered if they were off attacking more tasty targets like cows and sheep.

After breakfast and a shower she would spend an hour or so doing small jobs such as washing clothes or researching a topic. One morning she had to remove the stitches from her wound, a distasteful task, but one she managed without fuss, which surprised her.

A newsagency provided a detailed map of the region. Meg used a pencil to divide the Maleny and Montville townships and surrounds into sections. Each day she would explore at least one of those areas thoroughly, searching for her perfect house. Some properties came close to meeting her needs and she made note of those. Only the ones that had their own water and power supplies were considered.

Her daily search would last until at least mid-afternoon, and as her strength and stamina increased, she began extending her explorations until nearly nightfall.

One day she spent time exploring the lake which nestled gently in the hills between Maleny and Montville. She did an internet search and found it was called Baroon Pocket Dam and that it was stocked with fish, including Bass, Golden Perch and Mary River Cod. She suddenly longed for fresh fish and vowed to find a way to catch some.

In the main street of Maleny she saw a store that sold used books. Hoping she could find some information on fresh-water fishing she forced her way through a back door and began searching the shelves. A tome, 'The Complete Works of William Shakespeare' caught her eye, and she thought it might help fill in the long hours of night. A handyman's guide found on a different shelf felt like a godsend. Another book caught her eye. It was by a Vietnamese Zen Buddhist monk and when she opened it to a random page, she found words that immediately calmed and soothed her, and she knew she would read it often.

She eventually found a comprehensive guide to fishing which came in a folder divided into sections by coloured tabs.

Her dinners were often just ready-to-eat meals she'd take from the supermarket freezer section. She always took the most expensive, hoping they were more nutritionally sound than the less expensive ones. She also opted for the white meat and vegetable varieties. Maintaining her health had become important once she realised that, if she got sick, there would be nobody to help her.

Writing in her journal became an activity that she found positive in many ways. It cleared her mind before sleep. It meant she could keep track of dates, feeling that this was important somehow, and it also helped her work through problems and anxieties.

"There are so many things to worry about and sometimes I see the future as bleak and full of insurmountable problems. Maintaining a positive outlook at these times is hard.

Reading the book by the Zen monk helps a lot. He says I have to live in the moment, which means not worrying about the past (it's gone) or the future (why worry about what might not happen?) but instead to be grateful for what I have right now. I can list those things: a roof over my head, clothing, food and good health. I feel really lucky when I think about it in this way.

The monk also suggests that every morning on waking I should think about how lucky I am to be alive. I must meditate on this and vow to make the most of the next twenty-four hours.

When my marriage fell apart, I could have used some of this man's wisdom. On the other hand, I'm not sure I would have been in the right state of mind to understand it."

Catching her first fish in Baroon Pocket Dam came as such a shock to Meg that she nearly came to grief. As the fish jerked suddenly on the line, she let out a scream and then jumped to her feet, making the boat rock crazily from side to side. She lost her balance and sat suddenly, knocking the wind out of her lungs.

She had come across a boat house the previous day which, as well as a rowboat and canoe, also contained angling equipment. The boat house was part of another group of luxury cabins located at the edge of the dam. This resort also had a reception area and kitchen, but no restaurant.

Meg took note of what style of rods, reels and tackle were on offer and then looked them up in the fishing book when she got back to her cabin. She knew nothing about lures but learned quickly. An internet search suggested using live worms from the garden, and also to try fishing at dawn or dusk.

So the sun was just rising over the misty dam the next morning when she pulled the boat into the water. June in Montville is cold, especially at daybreak, so she shivered in the light track top she had put on while still half asleep. Her first attempts at rowing were comical, but she kept trying, and eventually found herself moving in the right direction.

She stayed on the dam for a little over an hour and in that time caught three fish. After rowing back to shore and pulling the boat high onto the bank, she walked up the hill to the kitchen she had seen earlier.

Wrinkling her nose, she gutted all three fish and threw one into a frying pan with a small amount of olive oil. When it was cooked through, she sat at the small, timber table and ate hungrily. The taste of the freshwater variety wasn't as clean as saltwater — it had a slight muddy and grassy taste, but it was enjoyable nevertheless.

While driving back to her cabin she turned the music up loud and used the steering wheel as a drumming instrument. She was in a high mood — fuelled by a sense of accomplishment — and as a celebration she decided to take the rest of the day off to just read and relax.

She danced through the restaurant and into the kitchen. The remaining fish were placed onto a plate before she opened the refrigerator to place them inside. She stopped, wondering what was different. No light. There was no light in the refrigerator. Saying, "No, no, no," she went to the light switch and hit it almost angrily.

Her carefree days were over. It was time to get serious.

CHAPTER FOUR

The four-wheel drive was handling the dirt roads with ease. Occasionally it would hit some corrugations which made the whole cabin shudder, but the ride was mostly comfortable.

Winter was the driest time for the southeast corner of Queensland. The days were blue, with pink and salmon tints at sunrise and sunset. The roads hadn't seen rainfall for some time, and Meg had to close the windows and sunroof to prevent dust from billowing into the cabin. Soon she had to reach for the air-conditioning controls as the winter sun beat through the windscreen. As she was doing this, she sensed rather than saw that she'd missed a driveway. She did a three-point-turn and headed back to where she'd just come from.

The driveway was narrow and rutted and climbed up a rise. Nothing much could be seen until she reached the top, but then she saw the house and smiled.

This was it — the house she had visualised right down to the smallest detail. It was low-set and sprawling with wide verandas and a large, open area at the front with a table and chairs. What made her heart beat faster was the sight of outdoor lights that had been left on. Electricity!

She scrambled from the car and walked past the outdoor furniture to the front door. It wasn't locked, but somehow she didn't expect it to be. The first section of the house was the living area with stained-glass windows set into the rammed earth walls. These sent playful beams of light dancing around the room. She moved further into the living area that was cool like a cave, and onward toward the rear of the house.

A smell, one she'd encountered often in the past few weeks, made her come to a stop. She sighed and covered the lower part of her face with the crook of an elbow before moving forward.

Like so many others, the house owners had died in their sleep. Their bodies were now covered in flies that were buzzing excitedly. Meg took one look and left the room, before opening all the windows and doors throughout the house. She then moved outside.

Her attention was first drawn to the livestock. There were a number of animals in various states of health. Meg could see that a windmill had been providing drinking water for those capable of reaching the trough it fed into, and the plentiful grass meant that those animals that relied mostly on this for food were unaffected by the lack of human attention. The chickens had all died, however, and Meg stood at the coop and sighed.

The roofs of the house and outbuildings were all covered with solar panels. Alongside the windmill that pumped water from the ground were two other, similar devices that had bigger vanes and were more modern. Meg had seen these in pictures of wind farms.

There were four large tanks being fed from the guttering on the various buildings. Meg knocked on the sides of the tanks in an attempt to determine their levels, but couldn't seem to find a difference in sounds.

The rear of the house had a view to the bottom of the property. There was a cleared section covered in grass, which was rich and lush. Surrounding that was bush which looked like it was still in its natural state.

On the far side of the house, Meg found, to her delight, a vegetable garden. It was well-established and covered in shade-cloth. Sadly the vegetables had been suffering through lack of water, and Meg quickly located a tap which was joined to the micro-watering system. The shadows were lengthening as the fine water mist began relieving the stress on the plants.

Meg counted twenty fruit trees which stood in neat rows in a section not far from the vegetable garden. They weren't bearing fruit so she had no idea what sort of trees they were, but there appeared to be a variety. There were also three banana palms.

She circled back to the outbuildings and began searching through them. One contained feed and equipment for the animals. Another housed a variety of machines. A third seemed to be the place to store any hazardous chemicals. The fourth came as a pleasant surprise — it contained a single bed, chest of drawers and a desk. A small refrigerator hummed in the corner. In the other corner, a door led to a tiny bathroom with shower. It was fairly clean — just needing dusting and sweeping — and she knew she could be comfortable there for the time it took to make the house habitable.

Back in the car she set the GPS to remember the location as 'Home' and then drove back to the resort to collect her possessions.

"It took a long time, but I have finally rid the house of the bodies. I began early this morning — as soon as the sun rose — and

I'm not going to relive the horror of that task by writing about it. I think it's sufficient to say that if this house doesn't end up being suitable for any reason, the next one will have to be empty of dead people. What a nightmare!

The bed had to be burned of course. I dragged it as far away from the house as I could and doused it in petrol before putting a match to it. Tonight I am sore, especially around the caesarean wound. I think I overdid it a bit.

Now the bedroom is empty and I'm trying to rid the house of the stench. I have lit some burners containing essential oils such as peppermint and ylang ylang. I wonder how long it will take to clear the smell.

It's nearly dark and I'm starving. I haven't eaten all day — haven't felt like it — and now realise I've made no plans for food. Surely there are some snacks in the car.

I just had a thought. The best bed in the world is in that cabin at the resort. I need a new bed. I wonder if I would be able to move it here. Perhaps by the time the smell leaves the bedroom, I'll be recovered enough to attempt it."

Every day Meg would try a new method of removing the smell from the house and gradually it receded until it was only noticeable if she closed the windows, which she only had to do once, when the unusually long, dry spell was broken by heavy rain and strong winds.

Still, it was six days until she could move into the big house, and the first night was spent in the spare room on an uncomfortable double bed. As she moved from side to side trying to find a firm place to lie on, she made the decision to take a bed from the resort on Obi Obi Creek.

The next day was spent on that task alone. A furniture truck was found — small so as to be easy to drive and manoeuvre. It had a furniture removal trolley in the back, which ended up being vital for moving the pieces of the bed to and from the truck.

Meg took sheets, blankets, pillows, towels, slippers and robes. The bedside tables and lamps were added to the haul. She raided the storage area and took boxes of the toiletries she'd enjoyed so much.

Once back at the house, she couldn't rest until the bed was in place and made up with sheets and blankets. Once finished, she stood at the doorway and surveyed the results with a smile. Only when it was perfect did she place Emily's bunny at the place where the pillows met.

She was beginning to worry about her sanity. Muttering to herself was becoming a habit and then some events had Meg concerned that she was in the early stages of paranoia.

It began one day when she was in the vegetable patch. She was removing the plants that had died from lack of water and was examining the rest for pests. As she straightened and stretched, she felt like she was being watched.

It was a sensation at the back of her neck, like a sort of prickling. Casually she turned around and looked behind her, but couldn't see anything. Later, as she was collecting potatoes, she felt it again.

She wondered how long it would be until she became insane, and thought of cases where people had been stranded on deserted islands and wondered how they had coped. She certainly didn't feel like she was going mad, but then she realised that perhaps the mad don't realise they are. She just hoped the sensation would go away.

Two days later the feeling was back. This time she turned quicker and thought she saw a flash of colour — yellow. It came from deep in the bush that bordered the property.

Later that afternoon, when she'd begun watering the trees in the orchard, she heard a dog growl and a snarl. There was a snapping of teeth. The dog yelped and whined. Then there was the sound of something moving quickly in the bush. She retrieved the .22 from the veranda and walked to the edge of the clearing. A figure wearing blue and yellow moved quickly out of sight.

Meg's heart began thumping. Could it be? Was it possible? She frowned for a moment and then made a decision. She'd seen a box containing a cake mix in the pantry. It only required water to make. She pre-heated the oven and mixed the batter with a wooden spoon. Soon it was in the oven and smells began wafting over the property.

The cake took fifty minutes to cook so in the interim she set up a small table and two chairs. A jug of cold water and ice cubes with slices of lemon came next and she added two glasses. When the cake was ready she cut generous wedges and piled them on a plate.

It didn't take long before she saw the blue and yellow flashes in the bush again.

"You may as well come out and share my cake. It's very good." Her voice squeaked from lack of use.

There was no response and nothing moved.

"It beats being attacked by dogs. I'm far less scary."

The bushes parted slowly. A figure emerged, that of a teenage boy, and he stepped through onto the grass. Although he was ten metres or so away, she could see he was in a sorry state.

Her first impulse was to run and embrace him, but

common sense told her to remain calm and lure him out like she would an injured animal. Smiling, she motioned him forward.

He kept most of his weight on one leg and looked at her through a long fringe. There was a bloody wound on his right arm that was fresh. He held a lump of wood like a club. Slowly he approached her.

She was right then, after all. She wasn't the only person to survive. The human population of earth was now double what it previously appeared to be. A lump rose in her throat.

Composing herself, she poured a glass of water and put it down on the part of the table that was closest to the other chair. She took a piece of cake for herself and bit into it. "Yum. Have some."

Actually the cake was awful, but she was sure he wouldn't think so. He wiped his hands on his pants and took a slice, eating it in large bites.

"If you haven't eaten for a while, take it easy to start with." He nodded.

They sat there silently for a few minutes while she tried to examine him surreptitiously. His shoes were worn through and she could see patches of reddened flesh poking through holes. His face was dirty and streaked with what she suspected were dried tears. She guessed his age to be around fifteen or sixteen. He looked like a character from a Manga comic — big eyes and a lock of black hair falling thickly past his eyebrows.

"I have a first-aid kit if you want me to look at that wound."

He bent his right arm and lifted it so he could see the damage.

"Dogs?"

He nodded.

"In that case we should act quickly. I should get some antiseptic cream on it."

He didn't say no, so she went to the four-wheel-drive and pulled out the first-aid-kit. It was in excellent condition.

By the time she returned, the boy had removed his shoes and was examining the sores on his feet. Mostly they were blisters, big and angry looking.

"Okay, I'd better treat those as well. I'll just go and get a bowl of warm water."

While the bowl was filling she thought about how the dog bite should be treated. Antibiotic cream and a tetanus shot?

He flinched as she cleaned and dressed the wounds but didn't say anything. She realised then that he hadn't spoken a word to her. She could only imagine what he'd been through. Did he find his parents dead? His siblings? What had made him set off on a journey on foot — one so arduous that he ended up with worn out shoes and large blisters? She thought of asking his name but decided to let him be silent for as long as he wished.

"Okay, that's about it for now. You'll need to stay off these feet for a few days. You can crash here if you want — there's a spare bed. For now you might want to have a wash." He nodded.

"I'm just going into town to pick up a few things. Is there anything you need?" All she got was an indifferent shrug.

"Okay, well I'll be back in a while. Make yourself at home."

Meg had no idea what a tetanus shot looked like, but figured that a doctor's surgery would have a supply of them. Sure enough, she was able to find two syringes marked 'Tetanus Toxoid' and took both, figuring she should also have one.

She found some dressings and bandages, as well as ointments and some scissors that were good for cutting dressings.

At a general store she bundled up some clothes,

pyjamas and other necessities. She saw a small axe, like a tomahawk and thought the boy should have it to protect himself from dogs. She also raided a DVD stand for some light movies.

Arriving home she found the boy lying on the sofa with his eyes closed, breathing deeply. She moved until she was directly above him and examined his features. She felt a gentle smile form across her face.

She had begun thawing a frozen chicken the day before, so was able to slide it into the oven. Carrots and potatoes from the vegetable patch would go nicely.

The boy slept through all the banging of pots and dishes in the kitchen and she was afraid he'd want to sleep right through dinner. As she was dishing the meal up she saw him stir and watched as he came to consciousness. At first his expression was unguarded and happy, but then his face suddenly changed, closing like the door to a safe.

"Dinner's in a couple of minutes — roast chicken and veggies, okay?"

She almost saw the hint of a smile.

"I found some DVD's. You can pick one out to watch after dinner. How about a bath while I wash the dishes and then we'll meet up at the TV?"

She felt that her attempts to provide him with some

semblance or normality were working. He seemed to be relaxing a bit.

"Oh, and I got you that little axe over there. It would be a good weapon against dogs." He hobbled over to the coffee table and picked it up. There was definitely a smile hovering around his mouth.

"But first we must eat. Come and help me with the plates."

"My father had type-one diabetes and needed constant insulin shots, so I know a bit about giving injections. I think it's important that you have a tetanus shot and I will have one as well." She let him digest that information for a few seconds.

"These have to go in the upper arm. Do you want me to do you first, or myself?"

He frowned for a moment and then pointed at himself. Meg was nervous but the result was good. The boy flinched but didn't cry out.

She had no idea how to inject herself. The angle was difficult but she got the serum in.

"Right. I think we deserved chocolate after that. What do you think?" She gave him a row of dark milk chocolate before helping herself.

The movie the boy had selected was a brainless action comedy which was not a genre she would normally enjoy. It was perfect for that first night, though, and the two hours went quickly.

The instinct to hug this traumatised young man was strong in Meg, and as she said goodnight she had to fight it, knowing it would be a mistake. She wished him a good night rather formally and watched as he limped into the spare room. Her emotions had been running at a heightened level in the hours since she discovered his existence, and this caused her to fall into a sleep that was deep but troubled.

Not long after midnight she woke with a thought running through her mind. Something didn't make sense. By the condition of the boy, she could tell he had walked a long way. Somehow he'd ended up at her house in Maleny, a house that was many kilometres from main roads and almost impossible to find accidentally. How had that happened?

CHAPTER FIVE

When Meg swung her legs out of bed the next morning, it was to find the boy sleeping on the floor where her feet were to go. Sometime during the night he had brought his pillow and blanket into the room and slept on the floor by her side.

Meg lay back down and examined his face. Peaceful in the morning light, it featured long eyelashes and olive skin. His eyes were closed but she remembered their brown depths from the day before. He was a good-looking young man and there was something about him that made her guess he was from wealthy parents.

Finally the need to use the bathroom caused her to move, and she shimmied to the other side of the bed and crept quietly across the timber floor. Using the second bathroom would be quieter than using the ensuite one, so she closed the bedroom door and made her way across the living room to the other end of the house.

This bathroom featured a full-length mirror which prompted Meg to undress and examine herself with critical eyes. Until that moment, the thought of her appearance hadn't crossed her mind — who would see her, after all? Now, though, there was another person in the world and she looked at herself as though through his eyes.

Her scalp was covered in around twenty days of hair regrowth and it looked patchy and ugly. Not having bothered with sunscreen in recent times had meant her complexion had roughened. Two eyes were sunken into hollow sockets and every millimetre of her skin needed both exfoliants and moisturisers.

Figuring that the boy would be more comfortable around her if she looked like a woman — his mother perhaps, she spent the next hour shampooing, shaving, removing dead skin cells and moisturising. Then she applied some light make-up, deodorant and perfume.

Meg's favourite t-shirt bore a smiley-face, so she teamed that with track pants and reassessed her image. The woman who stared back at her from the mirror looked younger and certainly more approachable.

It was time to cook them both some breakfast.

"I wonder where we could find some live chickens. Any ideas?"

The boy took a mouthful of cereal and shook his head.

"Hmm, somewhere with automatic feeders and an ongoing power supply. Poultry sheds. I'll look today. A hatchery too...some chickens might be just ready to hatch. I don't suppose you know how long it takes a chicken to hatch after the egg is laid?" The boy looked at her with a frown.

"Never mind...where's the tablet? Got it. Um...how long chickens take to hatch... ah...here it is...21 days."

She walked over to the journal and looked at the date. "Yesterday was the 7th June, so any eggs put in an incubator on 12th June would have hatched a few days ago. Anyway, I plan to hit some poultry farms today if you want to come along." He nodded.

"So, your clothes are in the bathroom and the blue toothbrush is yours. As soon as you're ready we'll go. I'll look up some addresses while you do that."

She found the details of three chicken farms, one close by, one in Landsborough and another close to Caloundra. Hopefully they'd get lucky at one of the closer ones. She had no idea what they'd transport the chickens in if they found any, but hoped the farms would have something suitable.

She looked forward to the day more than usual and realised it was because she had someone to share it with.

"What I know about chooks you could write on the back of a postage stamp."

They were pulling into the second poultry farm where they were greeted with the sounds of chickens cackling.

"But at least I know what a rooster looks like. I'll grab one of those and several hens — as many as we can carry in case some die."

The boy reached for the door handle but Meg stopped him. "You need to keep those feet clean. I reckon the stuff on the floor of the sheds will be full of chook poo and things. You'd best stay here."

What Meg learned in the next half-hour or so was how hard it was to catch and handle chickens, especially if you were trying to do it carefully so as not to scare them to death. She wished the boy was able to come and help her.

At one stage she was reaching in a big metal nest to remove a hen that was sitting there, when the cacophony of noise in the immediate area quietened. She looked around to see why and noticed that the hens had moved to allow a clear path for a rooster that was running at full speed toward her legs. She screamed and jumped backward, hitting the small of her back on the nests behind her. She swore.

In the end she had one rooster and five hens in some cages she'd found in an equipment area at the front of the shed. After placing those carefully in the vehicle, she went back for eggs, collecting twenty. She wondered if she could find a way to incubate them to produce more chickens but decided it might be too hard.

As they were driving back to the house she began trying to discover some information about her new companion.

"Hey, I don't think I've told you my name yet. It's Meg. It's Margaret, really, but no-one calls me that. My boss did, though." She fell silent.

The boy looked out the window.

"So what's your name, then?"

Silence.

"Let me guess. Rudolph?" She giggled. When there was no reply, she continued. "Wally? Warren? Archibald?" No reply.

"Well, if you won't tell me I'll have to make one up and call you that. How about Adam?"

He shook his head.

She sighed and they drove the rest of the way in

silence, except for the sounds of distressed chickens.

After settling the chickens and rooster into the coop, they went back into Maleny. The boy saw a sign to a shop that sold gourmet ice-cream and pointed. "Sorry, honey. They haven't had electricity for a long time. No ice-cream there."

As they passed a music shop she saw him gaze intently at the front window. "Do you play an instrument?" He just shrugged. She did a u-turn and pulled up right outside the store and then took her tools to the door and broke in.

The boy had clearly been taught the difference between right and wrong, and didn't quite know where this activity fitted in that scheme of things. "It's okay. We have special rights." His gaze fell on a guitar which he picked up quickly. "What can you play?" He strummed a few chords that sounded about right, but then seemed to lose interest. "Pick out some music — we can take it home with the guitar." He looked up with wide eyes and rummaged through the sheets quickly, picking several.

They raided a shoe store for sandals and running shoes for the boy. In another store they found some cotton socks. He stayed in the car while she went into the supermarket to find bread mix. It was time she baked some crusty loaves.

After she'd finished washing the dinner dishes she threw two big cushions onto the floor in front of the fireplace and dragged a coffee table between them. The pack of cards she'd found were the standard playing type and in good condition.

She began slowly, making one room with a roof and then adding another room. He placed the guitar against the wall, slipped off the sofa and crawled over, watching intently. She placed the card pack between them and he began copying her movements, adding to her building, but a bit clumsily so the structure soon fell. He looked at her as though checking for a reaction. She smiled and began again. Soon he had learned the subtle tricks necessary to avoid another collapse and they worked in companionable silence.

When they had finished the third story and started the fourth, she secretly moved a card at the base so the house of cards tumbled messily to the table top. She noticed his first reaction was one of mild humour, exactly what she'd been hoping for. Someone prone to temper or negativity would be hard to live with.

She slid a new DVD into the player and they began watching a popular animated movie. After an hour or so she noticed the boy had fallen asleep. She turned the movie off and found a blanket to cover him with.

Through the night a movement in her bedroom woke her. It was the boy, lying down on the floor beside her bed. She smiled and went back to sleep.

CHAPTER SIX

She let the boy sleep in for the first hour or so that she was awake. In that time she milked the cow and saw to other tasks that needed to be done daily.

When she returned to the house, she was surprised to find him awake and hunched over a map that he'd spread over the floor. He was mouthing words to himself and tracing his finger over roads heading north.

"Good morning. The cow gave us plenty of milk and the chickens seem okay, although they haven't laid any eggs."

He continued studying the map intently.

"Pancakes?"

He looked up and nodded quickly but quickly resumed looking at the map.

After breakfast she noticed him walking across to the

machinery shed. He pulled the doors apart and looked into the long, dark building. He opened more doors and soon had the whole front of the shed exposed. Then he went inside.

It was an outbuilding Meg hadn't given more than a cursory glance to, so she was surprised to see the boy wheeling a motorbike from it. It was a small one — a dirt bike, she thought. He stood it on its stand and went back into the shed.

Later she saw him with what looked like an owner's manual. He was sitting beside the bike comparing pictures in the book to parts of the machine. Later she saw that he had opened the shed that housed chemicals, and had taken out some lubricants. There was a piece of material spread across the grass, some tools laid neatly on top.

He worked on the bike all day with a concentration she was surprised he possessed, given his age and sex. Before nightfall she heard him try to kick the engine over, but it wouldn't quite start. He wheeled it back into the shed, tidied up the tools and returned to the house to clean up before dinner.

He wasn't interested in a movie. He booted up the old desktop PC in the spare room and spent time on the internet. Meg couldn't see the screen from where she was.

At bedtime she went to spare room to say goodnight.

He barely responded.

That night he slept in his own room.

The sound of a roaring engine shattered the stillness of the morning. Meg pushed the bedclothes back and stood quickly. She ran to the window.

The boy was on the motorbike, revving the engine and trying to move forward. His shoulders were tense and his mouth set in a straight line. Gradually he got the bike moving forward and did a lap of the house. He stopped and revved the engine, his head cocked to one side. He set off down to the end of the property and then returned.

Meg went out to the veranda and clapped. "Bravo!"

She was surprised to see that he didn't look happy from his achievements. It seemed he was more relieved.

That afternoon, as she stood up from weeding the vegetable patch a wave of dizziness made her unsteady. Not long after that she began feeling shooting pains in her joints and began shivering. By nightfall she was very ill.

Dinner was forgotten as she walked into the bedroom and fell across the bed. She pulled the blankets over herself and curled up into a ball. The boy came in and looked at her with raised eyebrows.

"I'm sick. I don't know what's wrong but it's bad.

Could you get me some paracetamol from the cupboard and a drink of water?"

After taking these she fell into a deep but troubled sleep.

For two days she mostly slept. Each time she woke she felt so dreadful that she would just swallow more paracetamol and water and burrow back under the bedclothes.

On the third day she woke feeling a bit better and worrying about the animals. Had the boy been milking the cow? Did he even know how to? Had he been looking after the chickens? She listened for signs of activity but there weren't any.

Her legs were unsteady, but she was able to stand and walk through the house. She splashed cold water on her face and drank thirstily. The animals were all where they should be and the chickens were active in the coop.

She heard a rustling in the spare room and went to investigate. The boy was in his bed, tossing and turning. His face was red and his skin looked hot. She placed a hand on his forehead and he opened his eyes. They were full of misery.

She fed him tablets and water and sat on his bed, wondering what it was that had afflicted them. She suspected a virus but wondered how they could have caught it.

Clearly the boy wouldn't be able to help with the chores, so she wrapped herself tightly in warm clothes and went out into the morning.

It was one of those perfect days that take the breath away. The sun was filtering through leaves that seemed greener than usual. There were patches of colour around, on animals and flowers and trees, and these seemed heightened. Meg stood in wonder, breathing deeply.

It was something she'd noticed since May 13th — since she'd woken up in hospital. It seemed that the colours of the world were brighter, more vivid. She likened it to when she'd once fiddled with a photo editing program and had turned up the saturation. Since everyone died, the world had become a more vibrant place.

The cow mooed, and that brought her back to reality. She took the milking bucket over to the feed shed and the cow followed her. Soon, milk from the overfull udder was being disgorged in hot streams. She rested her head against the cow's stomach and worked the teats until there was no more milk to come.

She fed and watered the chickens and walked around the property. Everything seemed all right. The dirt-bike was under the veranda, covered with a blanket. The windmill creaked lazily in the slight breeze.

She moved inside, drank more water and went back to bed.

A cacophony of noise woke her. There were dogs barking and animals squealing in distress. She shook her head, trying to clear the fuzzy feeling. She was still dressed, so she grabbed the rifle from the shelf by the back door, and ran straight outside.

A pack of dogs had surrounded the feed shed where the animals had congregated and were circling them, growling and snarling, while all the time moving closer.

Meg crept toward them, the rifle raised to her shoulder. She knew she had to wait until she had a clear shot; otherwise she might hit one of her animals. A large, mean looking German Shepherd swung out to the right, and she saw her chance. She aimed and fired, and the dog dropped to the ground.

The other dogs didn't seem to notice. There were five of them, mostly large breeds. She picked out the Labrador next, and it took two shots to fell it. The Border Collie went quickly. By this time the other dogs sensed something was wrong, and glared at her as she approached. She shot one more before the other two took off into the bush. She wondered how long it would take before they decided to return.

Fencing, they needed fencing.

She realised the noise hadn't brought the boy outside. The shadows and cooling air told her that it was late afternoon, so she hadn't seen him for hours. She moved inside and went to his bedroom.

His condition had deteriorated, and he looked smaller in the double bed. His skin was dry and hot. She noticed that he hadn't touched the water she had left on the bedside table.

The next few hours seemed like a nightmare to Meg. The boy was in a bad state, and she didn't know how to help him. She was still ill herself, and didn't feel capable of nursing him. She tried her best.

Around midnight she was afraid he was dying. His breathing had become so shallow she could hardly feel it. His skin was tight and burning. She kept applying cloths soaked in cold water to his face and chest but they didn't seem to be doing any good. She realised she would have to immerse him in cold water.

It took her several minutes to find the plug and start filling the bath. When she got back into the bedroom it was to the sight of the boy convulsing. She cried out and ran to him, holding him down. The convulsions passed after a minute or so.

"Don't leave me! You can't! I need you here. I've lost too many people and I just couldn't bear to lose you too. I don't know what I'd do. Please don't die!"

She lay beside him, stroking his forehead.

"I lost a boy just like you, you know. His name was Nicholas, but I called him Nicky. He was younger than you and had blue eyes, but you remind me of him. I can't bear to lose you as well."

She kept talking to him, telling him about her children and her previous life in that normal world. Once she began talking, the floodgates opened and all the repressed memories flooded back.

"Richard and I shared custody of Emily and Nicholas, and I didn't have them with me when everyone died. I guess that's a sort of blessing."

The boy's temperature seemed to be dropping, so she kept talking.

"Nicky was such a smart boy. Really good at maths. He loved sport, too, and played junior AFL. God, I miss him so much. And Emily, she was a little princess. She was into fairy costumes and dancing. She had just begun ballet lessons." Meg's voice broke. She cleared her throat and kept talking.

"Then I had another baby. The father was a photographer I met at a work function. His name was Craig, and he knew all the right words to seduce me really quickly. Other than my husband, he was the only other man I'd ever...well...you know... been with. It was never a proper relationship — he would just call me when he had some spare time and come to my house. I could never refuse him, although I felt I was being used. He never took me anywhere, or bought me any presents, or anything. He'd just come and eat the food I offered, drink any alcohol I had, and take me to bed. Then he'd just go and I wouldn't hear from him for days, sometimes more than a week.

"We had only been using condoms, nothing else. One of them obviously didn't work. When I found I was pregnant I was horrified. I rang and left a message on his phone to come and see me. He took two days to arrive and when I told him the news he got angry and accused me of trying to trap him. He insisted I have an abortion. I nearly did, but found I couldn't go through with it. When he discovered this he blew up and I never saw him again — well not until I saw him dead in my best-friend's bed.

"It was all for nothing anyway. The baby died, you see. He died while I was having him — just before everyone else died."

Tears had been streaming down her face. She wiped them angrily. The boy seemed a lot calmer. He was lying, breathing normally, and his face was a healthier colour. She heard the bath still filling and went to turn the taps off.

"My boss was really angry at me when I got pregnant. She'd been through several P.A's in the previous couple of years, mostly through them getting pregnant. She thought that I wasn't at much risk of that. I was recently separated from my husband and already had two children. She had been helping and mentoring me. She had placed me in training courses to improve my skills, and had invested a lot of time and money. I never mentioned Craig to her because it sounded too pathetic. When I became pregnant she really got angry. She said, 'It must be that bloody office-chair. Everyone that sits in it has a baby!' Eventually she calmed down, especially after I told her I didn't intend to leave her when the baby was born. I'd find someone to look after it."

She shifted position and lay beside the boy. Her eyes became fixed on the ceiling.

"Both the men in my life have been bad to me. Is it me, do you think? Is it a respect thing? My ex-husband was good to me to start with, when we were going out and in the early stages of marriage. Then he wanted to do an MBA so he could improve his prospects. That was just as Nicky was born. Richard would work all day and study at night. If Nicky cried, Richard would get angry and tell me that all he asked of me was to keep the baby quiet. We couldn't go out or have fun because he was studying so hard. It wasn't enough that he qualified; he had to get top scores.

"By the time Emily arrived and was walking around, he had earned his MBA with honours. He got a top job in a merchant bank and was suddenly earning enormous amounts of money. He worked long hours and also had to socialise a lot. We rarely saw him.

"One Christmas, the bank held a party that spouses and partners were invited to. It was a big deal and Richard told me to get my hair done and buy a new dress. I couldn't find anyone to mind the children so I went looking for an outfit with them in tow. Nicky threw a fit and we had to go home. I rang Mum and asked if she could look after them the next day. That was actually the day of the party. She said okay, as long as I took them to her house — she wouldn't have a car that day. So I drove two hours down to her place, went to a boutique in this small country town nearby and tried on a couple of outfits. The owner of the shop came to look and told me that one looked really good. It was the most expensive one. I was a bit doubtful — the cut seemed to accentuate my short legs and I thought I looked a bit too squarish in it. It also seemed old-fashioned, so I said I wasn't sure. The owner got someone else to come and give an opinion and they said it looked great so I bought it.

"The hairdresser had a tiny salon and had been cutting my mother's hair for years. We decided on a totally new look. It took a couple of hours. I grabbed the children from Mum's and drove home quickly.

"Richard took one look at my hair and outfit and threw a fit. I actually thought he was going to hit me. The babysitter stared at us with huge eyes and she must've thought we were quite mad. Richard made me change into another outfit I had which wasn't much better. At the function he barely spoke to me all night. After that, things got worse."

Meg swallowed heavily and felt the boy's forehead again. It seemed like the crisis had passed. She sighed and looked at the ceiling.

"Then he left me for someone else. Well, he didn't leave me — I was the one who had to leave 'cause he wanted the house. I moved into my Grandmother's place and that was that. All over. As quickly as that." She clicked her fingers.

"Do you think it's me?" She turned and looked the boy squarely in the face. "Do you think the men reckon I'm weak and exploit it?"

The boy's eyes had opened and he gazed at her

steadily. He reached for her hand and squeezed it. He felt cooler. He was going to be okay.

CHAPTER SEVEN

She woke to hear fingers hitting a keyboard and opened her eyes wearily. This wasn't her bedroom. Events of the night before came to her in a rush and she sat upright quickly. She was still fully dressed and lying on top of the boy's bed. He was at the desktop computer, his back to her, typing quickly and making noises of frustration.

"What's happening?"

He didn't look around but hit the desk with his fist and pointed at the monitor. He typed again and pointed, then did the same again. She saw what he was trying to tell her. The internet was failing.

She had noticed some early signs of it the last time she was researching a subject on the tablet. That was two or three days ago. It had worsened a great deal since then.

"Shit. Ah, well — it had to happen eventually. I guess

we were lucky it lasted as long as it did." The boy didn't look convinced. "We'll miss it badly though and things will get harder without it. I guess we'll have to start going to libraries and bookshops to find things out."

She thought about the times she had found quick answers just by typing a few words in a browser. How else could she have worked out how to milk a cow, for heaven's sake?

"How are you feeling this morning?" He gave her a thumbs-up.

"Something bad happened while you were out of it." She gave him a quick summary of the dog attack. "We're going to have to build an enclosure for the animals and really quickly. I'm going to drive down to that big hardware store at Maroochydore today and see what fencing materials they have." He nodded. "I'm also going to have to dispose of the dead dogs, but for now I might just drag them into the bush."

She lay back on the pillow for a moment, willing some strength to return. Perhaps a good breakfast would help both of them.

The four-wheel-drive had a towbar, and there was a trailer in the machinery shed. It took Meg some time to work out how to couple everything together, but soon they were driving to

Maroochydore with a list of materials needed.

The huge hardware store was a handyman's paradise. Even Meg became a bit excited about the possibilities many of the products suggested. They roamed the aisles with wide eyes for a while before Meg realised she still wasn't very strong, and that they should just get what they came for before her legs gave way. She marvelled at how quickly the boy had recovered.

With the trailer fully-laden, she took a slight detour to the beach, which wasn't far out of their way. She parked on a headland, and they watched the waves wash into shore and the seagulls wheeling through salt spray.

"We'll come back here soon and catch some fish. Maybe even set some crab pots. That would be fun, eh?"

The boy nodded and they drove home.

"Well, it isn't pretty but it will do until we can work out a better way." They were standing at the feed shed, looking at the haphazard fence they'd just erected.

Their logic had been sound. They had used the shed as one side of the enclosure and hammered some star posts into the ground at each of the front corners of the building. At intervals of three metres they had put more posts until they figured the enclosure would be big enough.

Then they attached chicken wire to the posts with fasteners, but at that point Meg saw a flaw in their design. "The dogs might be able to get under the wire." She had thought for a moment and then decided to dig a shallow trench that the wire could sit in. She began at one corner of the shed and the boy at the other side. They dug grimly in silence until they met halfway around.

Meg made them a late lunch which they ate quickly, surveying their work as they did so. The next part of the process was attaching the chicken wire to the posts all the way around. There was no gate, but that didn't matter as they could gain access through the back door of the shed.

The dirt they had dug from the trench was then put back around the base of the wire and flattened. "I guess the dogs could still dig underneath if they tried hard enough, but this will buy us some time."

Her plan was to let the grass-eaters out of the enclosure during the daytime while she and the boy were at home. At other times they would lead the animals through the shed, into the safe area.

Several times during the day she had noticed the boy gazing at the dirt bike. "Hey, why don't you go for a ride on the bike while I clean up and start putting some dinner together?" She didn't have to ask twice.

In the early hours of the next morning, Meg stirred, wondering what noise had woken her. It had come from the veranda. She dozed again.

A few hours later she sat up with a start. The sun was brighter than when she normally woke and she realised she'd slept in.

Still she didn't rush. She lay back on the pillows and thought about what the day would hold. They'd achieved so much in the day before that they could afford to take things easier. Perhaps fishing on Lake Baroon?

She couldn't hear the boy stirring. He'd worked well with her the day before and she wondered if he enjoyed it or just went along with her ideas out of a sense of duty. Why didn't he talk? Was he born that way? Was it induced by trauma? She'd resisted asking before now, but decided that the time had come. She could ask him questions and he could write replies.

With that thought, she rose and wrapped her robe tightly around her. The air was crisp. She moved into the living area and saw that the boy's bedroom door was open. The bed was empty. Unusual.

In the next few minutes she discovered that a number of things were missing: the backpack the boy had been using, as well as all his clothes, shoes, toothbrush and the first aid kit. She looked for the map he often pored over, but couldn't find it. Then she realised the bike had gone.

The sound that woke her in the early morning was probably him wheeling the silent bike from the veranda and down the driveway.

Desolation rose in her. He'd run off! He didn't want to be with her! Did she work him too hard? Were her meals not nice enough?

She realised that blaming her own actions in this case wasn't going to get her anywhere. It didn't make sense that a boy his age would leave a safe place with food and run away. No, it had to be something else.

The map. He had been looking at the road north to Cairns.

Not stopping to get changed she ran out to the four-wheel-drive and started it quickly. There was only one main route leading north, so she took it and sped along the roads. She figured he had a head-start of several hours, but the dirt bike wasn't designed for long stretches of high-speed riding. She'd catch him.

It didn't take long. Rounding a corner she had to brake suddenly to avoid the bike that was lying across the road. A few kilometres further she saw the boy walking determinedly, but with a limp. As she pulled up beside him she realised her heart was beating faster than usual. She also knew she had to handle this situation carefully if she wanted a good result.

"Hey ... I guess you're trying to head to Cairns. Is that right?"

He kept his eyes forward, striding purposefully.

"Did you know it's about the same distance as going from Melbourne to Maleny? On foot it will take you weeks. If you get there."

His walk slowed.

"Is it really important? That you get to Cairns?"

He nodded vigorously.

"Okay, I'll help you. Hop in and I'll look on the GPS and tell you how long it would take in this car."

It was about eighteen hundred kilometres. "That's a couple of days driving. We'll go back and sort something out for the animals and do other stuff. How about we leave the day after tomorrow?"

He frowned and shook his head.

"Okay, tomorrow at first light. We'll have to drive hard because we can't leave the animals for too long."

CHAPTER EIGHT

Google Maps was still working and it told Meg that she could get to Trinity Beach, the suburb north of Cairns that the boy indicated on the map, in eighteen and a half hours non-stop. Clearly she wouldn't be able to drive all that distance without resting, but she'd do her best to get there as quickly as possible.

As she sat looking at the map on the tablet, she thought about fuel. She had been plain lucky so far, but couldn't count on a regular supply on this trip. What methods could I use? Syphoning from other cars?

She'd seen her father do it on farm machinery, but that was the total of her knowledge. The handyman's guide was an old book, but it had some information on the subject. Apparently the idea was to have a hose you could see through to save getting a mouthful of petrol. Ugh.

A conversation she'd overheard in the lunch room at work came to mind. One of her co-workers wanted to transfer some fuel from his wife's car to his for some reason. He found it was impossible because of some sort of mesh grid that had been added to the filler of modern cars to prevent petrol theft. Meg wondered which year this was introduced.

She rocked back in her chair and bit her lip. This was going to be a big problem, not only on this trip but ongoing. She decided to come up with a workable solution there and then to save problems in the future.

She thought about pumps she'd seen her father use on 44-gallon drums on the farm. Could one of these be used to pump fuel from underground tanks of service stations? Perhaps adapt one? She knew there were outlets that sold pumping equipment.

She hadn't used the Yellow Pages in years — no need with the internet. Now, however, she had to search through cupboards and felt lucky to find one of the thick books. The closest pump shop was Nambour. They'd call into there at the start of the trip in the morning.

Wet roads are frustrating when high-speed driving is

imperative. She took a few risks, but the four-wheel-drive was in good condition and she trusted it. She had already checked the tyre tread and pressure, and the fact that the vehicle was equipped with anti-skid brakes was of huge benefit to them.

As she sipped from the first of two thermoses of strong coffee, her mind whirled. She was totally baffled about the reason for the trip and had no idea what was going to happen when they arrived at their destination. Was the boy planning on staying in this place? How would she handle that? Would she try to stay with him?

They saw signs to major towns flip past them: Noosa, Maryborough, Hervey Bay, Bundaberg and Rockhampton. At Mackay they were faced with the choice of finding fuel or using some from the jerry cans. It made sense to put the new pump to the test.

They stopped at a service station and walked around with their heads bowed, scanning the concrete driveway until they discovered a metal plate that gave them access to the tanks. It was difficult to remove, but a crowbar Meg was carrying in the back of the vehicle helped.

"Damn it!" There was a second level of access to the tanks, and this was secured by a lock that seemed impenetrable. Meg flung the back door of the vehicle open and took out the door-bashing tools. The boy helped her gain access to the attendant's console and eventually he found the key in a drawer. Meg closed her eyes in relief.

The new pumping system worked well. They were able to completely replenish their fuel supplies, the only problem occurring as they drove back onto the main road. The pump filled the car with fumes. They pulled it out again and drained the hoses thoroughly. They wiped it with rags. There was a small improvement. In the end they just opened the sunroof and all the windows and put up with it.

By the time they left Mackay it was mid-afternoon and they had covered around nine-hundred kilometres. After another hour of driving, they pulled up at a rest stop and they shared some snacks and water. Meg wondered if she should have a nap but decided to push on. She drank more coffee, turned the music up loud, smiled at the boy and hit the road again.

As she crossed the river on the outskirts of Townsville she felt a weariness come over her. She had been driving for nearly fourteen hours, and had covered more than twelve hundred kilometres. There was a pain in her lower back, and her legs felt cramped.

They pulled into a parking lot at the foreshore and gazed at the sea that resembled a sheet of tin. The Great

Barrier Reef and Magnetic Island acted as coastal protection — no surf.

The sun was sinking into the horizon behind them, giving the atmosphere an unreal quality which was made more pronounced by the stillness and silence.

Meg opened the refrigerator in the back of the four-wheel-drive and pulled out a package of food. She and the boy stared into the orange-lined clouds and ate thoughtfully. When the last bite was taken, she aimed the wrapping at a bin which was only three or so metres from the car and threw it. The result made her laugh and clap. "A hole in one!"

She turned to the boy. "We'd better have another look at the map." He pulled it from his backpack and passed it to her. She found Trinity Beach and looked at it closely.

"Okay, well because I'm such a brilliant driver, we're now only five or so hours from Cairns. I need to know exactly where we're going. Trinity Beach looks like some sort of housing estate — like those blocks of land that have marinas attached. Where should we go when we get there?"

He frowned and shrugged. Then he put his hands together and leaned his head on them — the universal sign for sleep.

"Yeah, I know you're tired. I'm exhausted — but where are we headed?"

He made the same sign again. She looked at him with her eyebrows raised.

He pointed his finger in the air and mimed the sleep action again. Then he pretended to wake up and then pointed to the map and nodded.

"You'll have a sleep and then you'll know? That's crazy."

He nodded excitedly.

"Well, okay. It's your ballgame, as strange as it is, so we'll play it your way."

The boy pushed his seat back.

"You can hop in the back, might be more comfortable. I'll just lay my seat down like this. Don't wake me — I'll just nap until I wake naturally." It wasn't long until they were both sleeping soundly.

The first rays of the sun hit Meg straight in the eyes. She winced and reached for the sunglasses, a movement which caused her knotted muscles and tight joints to rebel. They hadn't liked the car seat.

The boy's face in repose was relaxed. He was breathing deeply. She attempted to open the door quietly, but it still made a loud noise. The boy was oblivious.

She walked down to the sand and began stretching,

ending with the yoga sequence Salute to the Sun, which seemed fitting at that time of the morning. She jogged a short way up the beach, loving the freshness of the morning. She felt energised again.

There were some mandarins in the back of the car. Meg had witnessed the fruit ripening on a tree in the orchard and picked some for the road trip. Now she peeled the loose skin and bit into a segment. Not the best she'd ever had, but it held the magic of coming from her own tree. She also ate a peanut butter sandwich and sculled a black coffee.

She spied a tap dripping listlessly into a puddle on the grass. With toothbrush in hand, she turned the handle and gasped when the water gushed suddenly into the puddle and exploded onto her bare legs. She adjusted the flow before washing and tooth-brushing. Suddenly she felt ready for the day, whatever it might bring.

Back in the car she saw her journal poking reproachfully from the top of her bag. She hadn't made an entry since before her illness. She pushed the temptation to begin driving aside and opened the book to a fresh page.

"*What will the day bring? I must admit to some nervousness, not knowing what this trip is all about. Why can't he just write things down for me — give me answers in writing? I believe his lack of speech is psychological because he also refuses to communicate in any manner unless he needs me to do something for him.*

I suppose I should be patient. Heavens knows what he's been through. I'm scared that if I push him too hard he'll run away. I nearly lost him two days ago. I don't want that to happen again.

If we get to this place at Trinity Beach and he wants to stay then so be it. I will go back to Maleny. Unless he asks me to stay and I'll have to think about that.

The weird thing is that I don't think he's been to this place before — so why is he so driven to get there?

He's waking now. I'll give him a few minutes to refresh himself then we'll drive the five or so hours and I'll know what the future holds for both of us."

Meg watched the boy wake fully. He jerked upright and immediately grabbed for the map. His finger traced places around Trinity Beach but after a minute or two he pushed the map onto the seat in frustration.

"Good morning. What's up?"

He climbed over the centre console and dropped into the passenger seat. He held the map under her nose, but then changed his mind and began fiddling with the GPS. Within a few seconds it was showing a new destination: 10 Brindabella Quay, Trinity Beach.

"Ah, good. We know where we're going then. Get cleaned up and grab breakfast and we'll be on our way."

Superman couldn't have got through his morning toilette as quickly as the boy did. It was like watching a movie in fast-forward. It seemed like only seconds before he was back sitting beside her and looking ahead expectantly.

"Well, okay then. I guess we're ready to go." She turned the key.

CHAPTER NINE

They hadn't struck any major traffic problems on the whole trip — until they arrived in Cairns. Two prime movers with large loads had come together and the result was catastrophic. One looked to be carrying something inflammable, while the other had a load of chickens, now dead.

These wrecks were blocking the road in both directions and Meg had to backtrack a long way to get around them. The detour lost them nearly an hour, and she could sense the boy's frustration.

It was around midday when they finally approached Trinity Beach. It seemed like a brand-new estate, tailor-made for boat owners. The houses were large and well-built. Brindabella Quay was on a small, man-made piece of land, jutting into the water.

Many blocks were still vacant, and others were either under construction or newly completed.

Number ten fell into the second category. Some new landscaping was evident — small bushes had been planted along the driveway, but had died through lack of care.

Meg had barely come to a stop before the boy jumped from the car and sprinted to the house. He knocked first but when there was no reply, quickly turned the door knob and ran inside. Before Meg had a chance to stretch her legs, he was out again, carrying something that looked like a bundle of clothing. As he approached, Meg saw tears running down his cheeks and moved to him quickly, realising that the object in his arms was a girl or young woman.

The boy laid her on the back seat, and Meg checked her vital signs. The heartbeat was rapid and thin, the respiration shallow. She looked half-starved and her eyes were sunken and dark-rimmed.

Dehydration? Starvation? Her mind went to all the medical shows she used to be so fond of.

"Okay, I'm going to a hospital to see what we can get for her. Try to give her sips of water, but not so quickly that she chokes. If she can't swallow, we'll try something else."

Cairns Base Hospital sprawled along a section of land which

lay opposite a beach. The car park was nearly empty, and Meg was able to select a parking space under a tree. She also kept the car running and the air-conditioning flowing into the back seat.

She ran up to the main entrance to the Emergency department, but found the automatic doors wouldn't open. Cursing, she looked both left and right for alternatives before finding a manual door fifty metres away.

It must have been a quiet night in Emergency when everyone died. There were several bodies scattered about, but they mostly appeared to be medical staff. Meg did her best to ignore the smell, and began checking cupboards and shelves. She found a plastic basket and began filling it; saline drips, tourniquet, thermometer, blood pressure gauge, IV line and antiseptic wipes.

She searched her memory for information on what to give an unconscious person who needed nutrition urgently — something that could be delivered via IV drip. She couldn't think of anything, so left the hospital.

"I don't know how to insert an IV line and I reckon it would be a silly question to ask if you do?"

His eyes widened and he shook his head.

"Well, I reckon that if we don't get this drip into her soon, she'll die. I'll just have to do the best I can."

Meg tied the saline bag to the handle above the passenger side door and then had a look over it for clues on how to use it. She slid the I.V. line into the base of the bag where it looked like it might belong, but then noticed that nothing had begun to drip into the clear chamber. This chamber was soft, so she squeezed it and it filled to halfway. Then the drip began.

Next she looked for any air bubbles. There were a few so she ran them down to the end of the tube. The boy was peering over her shoulder which was distracting, so she suggested he cradle the girl's head in his lap and talk to her.

She figured the next logical step was to insert the line into a vein. She tied the tourniquet around the girl's wrist and waited for a vein on top of the hand to swell. Nothing happened so she assumed it might be because of dehydration. She closed her eyes and took a deep, shuddering breath. Then she gently slid the needle of the line into what she hoped was a suitable vein.

She could see the blood flowing back into the plastic tube. She pulled the needle back a fraction and laid the tube flat. Meg's hands were shaking as she fiddled with a wheel halfway up the line that appeared to adjust flow. She taped the needle into place and straightened.

"I dunno. I've tried my best. What we should do now

is drive her back to Maleny as quickly as possible. We can take better care of her there. Is that what you want?"

He stared down at the girl and stroked her hair. When he looked up again there were tears in his eyes. He nodded.

"Okay then. You stay here in the back and keep supporting her head. Keep an eye on the saline solution and let me know when it's nearly empty so we can replace it. Damn, I need petrol. Okay, let's go."

When Meg had driven at the exhaustive pace to reach Cairns quickly, it was before she knew she would have to make the return trip even faster. She just drove and drove and drove, becoming almost hypnotised by the road.

"When I look back on that drive from Cairns to Maleny it seems unreal, like a fantasy. I don't recall hardly any of it. Twice I almost ran off the road after nodding-off to sleep, and on both of those occasions I stopped and had a short power-nap. Then I drove some more."

In Mackay they stopped at the same service station they used on the northbound trip. Refuelling proved to be quick and easy and when they were finished, they parked under the awning covering the pumps and ate some of the food they'd packed. It was never intended for a return journey and was beginning to taste stale, but they ate it quickly anyway.

Around an hour south of Mackay, the GPS flashed a message that the satellites could not be reached. Meg fiddled with some settings before re-booting the system. Nothing worked. She turned, got the boy's attention and tapped the screen where the message was displayed. "I guess it had to happen eventually. We'll have to use maps from now on. At least I know the way home."

Occasionally Meg would turn around or look in the rear-vision mirror to see how the two in the back were travelling. The boy held the girl's head gently and would occasionally move a greasy strand of hair from her face. One time Meg saw him peel a mandarin and place it to her lips and she stirred just enough to swallow some of the juice. It was the only food or drink the girl seemed interested in.

Meg changed the saline drip bags often and hoped this was enough to keep her alive until they arrived home. She had no idea how she'd treat the girl once they arrived there and wished they had some comprehensive medical books.

It had been around four o'clock in the afternoon when they left Cairns. They finally pulled into the driveway at Maleny at four-thirty the following afternoon. As they approached the house, Meg calculated that it was day thirty-seven of the new world order.

She had driven more than three thousand, six hundred kilometres in two and a half days. When she opened the door of the car and dropped to the ground, her legs almost gave out.

"I woke just now to a thrilling sound — one that has made my heart beat faster and put a smile on my face. It is the sound of another voice.

Even though the girl is in the spare room, I can hear her clearly. Her voice is girlish and although I can't make out the words, I can tell she is speaking very fast.

I should get up and see her — check her vital signs and general condition — but it's so nice just lying here quietly.

She's giggling now, the girl. Now she's chattering again and it doesn't seem to worry her that it's a one-sided conversation. Her voice trills up and down scales and has variances in volume and tone.

I can't wait any longer — I've got to see what the boy thinks of all of this."

Meg rolled out of bed and padded silently through the house, stopping next to the door of the spare room. From there she slowly moved her head until the bed came into sight. She needn't have been furtive — the two of them were oblivious to her.

The girl was lying in much the same way that she and the boy had laid her the afternoon before, except that there were now three pillows under her head. The bed was littered with food scraps and packaging.

The boy was seated on the bed, looking down at her with an expression of dazed wonderment. He was following every word as though they contained the secrets of the universe.

"So, I didn't give up, really. I really hoped you'd still come. But I sort of lost interest in everything for a while, but then you came and now I'm really, really happy!"

Meg cleared her throat and two heads swivelled around to look at her.

"Good morning, you two. Did you sleep well?"

Meg had a great many questions to ask, but thought the gentle approach might mean she eventually received quality answers.

"Oh, yes thank you. And also thanks for all that you did to rescue me. I don't remember much except Luke here feeding me mandarins." She laughed, the strange tinkling sound echoed through the house.

Luke? The boy's name was Luke?

"I'm Meg, by the way. What's your name?"

"Oh, sorry. Of course you don't know yet — silly me! Meg is a nice name by the way. Mine is Constance. It's old fashioned I know but it was my grandmother's name — on Mum's side." Her eyes began to fill with tears. She cleared her throat. "Anyway, my best friend calls me Connie. Well, she used to..." The tears began coursing down her cheeks.

"Connie is a lovely name. So how long have you and Luke known each other?"

She blinked at Meg several times.

"Oh, just since — well, just now really."

"Just now?"

"Yeah, well as I said, I sort of remember him looking after me on the way here, but I'm only just really getting to know him now."

"Ah, okay. So I must've missed something here. He knew where to find you and you know his name. How?"

She looked at Luke and he nodded.

"This is gonna sound really weird, you know? We both had dreams, sort of. About each other and stuff like that. My dreams were all about him coming to get me. Just now I asked him if he had dreams about where I was and he nodded."

Meg was having trouble believing this until she thought of her own dreams — Richard telling her that the

Sunshine Coast hinterland would be a good place to live, and also how she woke with the exact knowledge of how the house would look. Luke finding his way to the Maleny house was still unexplained as well. Did he dream of that?

"We'll have to compare notes later about all these things, but for now I'll have to check you over. Luke — seeing as you're now the man of a household with two women, you can feed the animals while I look after Connie." She thought she saw an almost imperceptible puffing of his chest as he left the room.

Meg took his place on the bed and reached for Connie's left hand. The puncture mark where she had inserted the I.V. line was red and angry looking.

"I'll get some cream for that. Does it hurt much?"

"No, well — just a bit. It throbs every now and again. You connected me to a bag through this?"

"Yeah, and we were lucky it worked well. Are you still hungry? I can see Luke's been feeding you."

"I was starving, you know? It hit me early in the morning. I just couldn't get enough to eat. Now I'm stuffed. I feel yucky, though. Dirty. My hair is awful."

"Are you up for a bath or shower, or do you want me to wash you here in the bed?"

"Oh, I'd love a bath! I love water, you know? I swim

a lot. Dad calls me his little fish...well, he used to. He'd take me out in his boat and I always wanted to swim when he was trying to catch fish." More tears welled.

"Right, I'll run you a nice warm bath then. I'll find you clean pyjamas or a nightie. Then you can come back here to bed for the rest of the day."

"Oh, good! I'd like that. Is there some nice smelly stuff to put in the bath? I think I smell bad. I always like to smell really nice, you know? Like flowers or candy or something. I have lip gloss that tastes like marshmallow. It's my favourite. My best friend — she really likes it too. When I buy one, I always get another one to give her."

Gosh the girl could talk.

"Yeah, I'll find something nice to put in the bath."

As Meg turned on the taps and watched the water gush into the bath, she realised that the novelty of someone else's voice had run its course. She found she preferred silence.

"I always brush my hair fifty times before bed, you know. My Grandma, Constance that is — the one I was named after — she taught me that. She said it massaged the scalp and helped the hair grow thick and shiny. So I do it all the time. Do you like my hair?"

"It's very nice, Connie." The girl looked completely different now that she was re-hydrated, fed, and washed. She had long, kinky, reddish hair and pale skin. There was a fine dusting of freckles across her nose and cheeks. Her eyes were large and blue.

"What happened to your hair?"

Meg laughed.

"It used to be long and thick like yours. When I got married and had children I got it cut shorter."

"Gee, you really cut it short all right!"

"Yeah, well I ended up shaving it all off." She desperately wanted to find another topic of conversation before Connie asked what prompted that extreme action. "So you smell nice again and you've got a book. I've got to catch up on a whole lotta jobs, but I'm sure Luke here will be happy to stay by your side."

"Oh, that would be sooo nice. I think Luke is my new best friend and he's sooo nice to me. It's just good to have someone to talk to again. I had no-one for so long."

"That must've been hard," Meg muttered under her breath as she left the room.

"*I have woken to silence, a blissful state that is rare at the moment.*

120

I don't know what to think about having Connie here. I mean, it has to be a good thing that someone else is alive — right? Has to be good that we saved her life? Luke is a lot happier — his face shines when he listens to her. It's just that it's so noisy now, after all that silence. When it was just Luke and I the house was a place of peace. Now there are shrieks and squeals and high-pitched laughing all the time. And talking...non-stop talking.

It is driving me insane.

Often when I find myself in a quandary, I think of my boss and say, 'How would Angela handle this?' She had a talent for summing up a difficult situation and then quickly positioning herself so the outcome would work to her advantage. I was constantly surprised by the successes she achieved this way. Some of her methods were breathtaking in the scope of the risk involved, and when I would comment on her skill, she would say, 'Fortune favours the brave, dear girl. Don't ever forget that.'

I have seen her make friends with people who seemed destined to be enemies, especially competitors in business. She would even offer these people help and advice. Her reason for doing this? 'Keep your friends close, and your enemies closer, Margaret.'

Her strengths lay in the fact that she was a people-person. She would remember the names, birthdays and troubles of every person she'd met. She would take time to talk to most people whether they were cleaners, shop assistants, or delivery persons, and would listen to their stories.

Originally a training school for office workers, her business expanded to job placement. I had signed up for several courses at the school to bring my skills to a level where I could re-enter the workforce and support myself. When it came time for job placement, I completed the psychometric test that all graduates did and the results became known to Angela. She plucked me from the pool of job-seekers and plonked me behind a smart desk outside her office which was equipped with state-of-the-art equipment.

It wasn't just the fact she was my mentor in every meaning of the word, she seemed to consider me her pet project. She was forever poking around in my psyche for remnants of damage left by Richard's treatment of me, and helping me let go of it.

One day she strode out of her office and said, "C'mon. We're going to lunch." I had only a second to grab my handbag before running after her, and soon we were in a cab going to her favourite business restaurant. Someone was already at the table and Angela introduced her as 'my good friend, Elizabeth.' As it turned out, this woman was a child psychologist and, as the lunch progressed, she drew details about my children from me. I blurted out the issues I was having with sharing custody with Richard and especially his new live-in girlfriend.

Elizabeth gently explained what damage can be done to children in custody battles and how to avoid it. She made me realise I didn't own Nicholas and Emily and that I should just step back from the battles and look at it afresh. 'There are three things to remember: Never criticise your ex or his girlfriend in front of the children — it causes loyalty issues; make the children feel like they can see you whenever they want; show them you can be happy on your own and that your happiness doesn't depend on them being with you.'

I came away from that lunch with a whole different mindset. That night I rang Richard and removed any barriers to the shared custody arrangement. For a long time I thought how lucky I was that Elizabeth had been at that lunch, before I realised that Angela had orchestrated the whole thing.

So what would Angela do if she found herself in my situation? How would she handle Connie? Firstly she would find out a lot more about the girl and what happened on the night of May 13th. She would talk to her for a long time — no, not talk, listen. She would hear the words that weren't spoken, understand the meaning of the gaps and silences. She would listen actively and not interrupt until Connie ran out of words. She would then take time to process this information — a day or two, before having another talk with the girl and coming to some sort of understanding.

And even while writing this, I have developed a theory. Maybe she didn't always talk this much. Maybe Luke's mutism and her chattering come from the same place — terrible trauma. I must investigate this.

The Zen monk tells me that unhappiness is caused by wanting something to be different to the way it is. It's up to me to change the way I view this, accept it so we can make our own happy little family."

Meg replaced the cap on the fountain pen with a smile. Writing about the problem had helped, and she was now committed to doing her utmost to ensure that the three of them remained harmonious.

CHAPTER TEN

"Hey, Meg!" Connie was walking across the grass, pulling Luke behind her. Both their faces were bright and flushed. "Guess what?"

"What?"

"We both had the same dream last night. It was a voice telling us that we must become man and wife."

Meg raised her eyebrows. "Really?"

"Yeah. It was, like an order or something."

"So what do you think it meant?"

Connie frowned. "I thought it was obvious. We have to get married!"

Meg thought that it could also have another meaning — just to have sex — but she didn't say so.

"Aren't you happy for us? Say something!"

"Of course I'm happy for you. As long as this is what

you want."

"Oh yes, isn't it Luke?" He smiled and nodded.

"I guess you're old enough — in some cultures you would have been married years ago. Anyway, it's not up to me. I'm not the mother of either of you."

"Yeah, but we want you to be happy about it. Besides, you'll have to perform the ceremony."

Meg laughed. "Yes I guess so. Have you picked a date yet?"

"Well, we've been awake for ages thinking about it. How about sometime romantic like the next full moon?"

"When is that?"

"On the nineteenth."

"The nineteenth of September 2013. It has a nice ring to it. A spring wedding. How exciting!" Meg was sounding more enthusiastic than she felt.

Connie hugged her. "Gee, thanks Meg. It means a lot to us."

As she watched the two of them run back into the house to make plans, Meg considered what feelings were welling up in her. It was mostly unease. It felt like there was a puppet master somewhere pulling strings, and the three of them — Luke, Connie and she — were dancing to his tune. Go to Maleny, find this house. Luke, walk and wreck your feet and get chased by vicious dogs, but get to the same house. Both of you drive thousands of kilometres to rescue Connie. Luke and Connie, become man and wife. What next?

It was weird and freaky, and she didn't like it. How could they be manipulated in this way? Who was pulling the strings? God? Did He just decide one day to kill off the population of the world, saving only three people and then manoeuvre them until He was satisfied with the result?

What other explanation could there be? Meg began feeling that terrible sensation deep inside of her, the same one she had when she first found herself alone. The one she was sure would result in madness if she let it.

There was only one thing to do. Go with it. See where it led. What other choice did she have?

Despite her misgivings, Meg went to a lot of effort to give Luke and Connie a memorable wedding.

On a shining blue spring day, they drove to a lookout along the ridge, from where the Glasshouse Mountains looked so close it seemed you could reach out and touch them. Meg had suggested this place, not only for the views, but because it had a pretty white gazebo which she had secretly decorated with ribbons and flowers early that morning. Connie gasped and clapped when she saw it.

The wedding ceremony itself was simple. When it came to the vows, Meg asked Luke if he wished to take Connie as his wife and lifted an eyebrow. She hoped his speech would return on this special day, but he simply nodded.

Meg had created a wedding certificate in a publishing program on the desktop computer. It looked authentic. Luke and Connie signed it with great seriousness and Meg added her signature as witness.

The food had been waiting in coolers and Meg began to unload items onto the picnic table in the gazebo. She had found a linen tablecloth and some silverware that she had polished to a shine. There were glass flutes beside an ice-bucket which contained French champagne. Last, but by no means least, a wedding cake that Meg had baked and decorated secretly in the dark hours of morning.

When she looked back on the images later, she saw it looked like a normal wedding celebration, the only difference being the lack of guests. The bride and groom were glowing with happiness and looked destined for a happy marriage.

When all the food had been eaten and the champagne drunk, Meg told them of the next surprise. She had gone to the resort where she had first stayed on her arrival in Maleny and selected another empty cabin. She had filled it with candles and coolers full of food and drink. There was a special nightdress lying on the bed among scattered rose petals.

She drove them there and handed Luke the key. "Don't forget to carry her over the threshold. I'll come and collect you the day after tomorrow. There's no power, but I don't think you'll mind."

'I'm alone now for two days and my God, it is so peaceful. I must say it's a bit strange though. I've sort of gotten used to having Connie to talk to.

She has a new maturity which has brought with it a different demeanour. Gone is the giggling, chatty girl. In her place we have a woman who is more, shall I say, dignified? Perhaps that's the wrong word. She's a lot easier to live with, anyway.

Her story of the night of May 13th was harrowing. She had slept late and woke wondering why. Normally her mother or sister would have been knocking on the door. She went to her sister's room first and found her not breathing and with a fixed stare. Connie screamed and ran into her parent's room to find them in the same state.

The girl next door went to her school and Connie knew her parents. She ran over to their house and pounded on the front door. When there was no reply she went around the back and broke in. There wasn't anyone alive.

Like me she tried television, radio and the internet for answers.

She thinks she went into a state of shock — remembers being very cold and shaking and doesn't know how long this lasted.

When we found her, everyone else had been dead for thirty seven days. Although her father had spoken about driving lessons, these had never happened, and she was too scared to drive. The housing estate was remote from other areas of Cairns.

When she ran out of food in her house, she began raiding the neighbours' pantries and refrigerators. When the estate lost power, she began to realise the full seriousness of her situation. That's when she began dreaming of Luke coming to rescue her. These dreams were so real that she didn't doubt it would happen.

But time went by and he didn't arrive. She got very ill with what she suspected was severe food-poisoning. After that her decline was rapid. She remembers moving to near the front door, her suitcase ready beside her so that Luke would find her quickly. We arrived just in time.

I don't know Luke's story, but I guess it is very similar. It's hard enough to find that everyone has died — everyone that you knew and loved — but added to that is the fight for survival. In our case — Luke, Connie's and mine, it wasn't as desperate as if we had been marooned in a desert without food or water, but it was still difficult, especially for the young ones who had never had to fend for themselves.

Now those same young ones are honeymooning and I discover I'm very happy for them."

CHAPTER ELEVEN

"Okay, Luke. Are you ready for a huge day of work?"

They were sitting around the breakfast table which was laden with pancakes, poached eggs and cereal that Connie had prepared. Luke nodded. Meg passed him more pancakes. "Eat up, you'll need the energy."

Maleny's usual high rainfall had been noticeably absent from the time Meg had first moved into the house to the day after the wedding. Once it started, though, it made up for lost time. They saw fifteen consecutive days of showers, followed by two clear days and then another nineteen days of downpours. They had woken that morning to the sight of blue skies and sunshine and now it was time to catch up on the outside jobs.

"Great pancakes, Connie. Your cooking is getting better every day. The eggs are perfect too. I love the runny yolks. Here, have one."

As Connie looked at the plate of eggs, Meg saw the colour drain from her face. "I...I just have to...."

Meg and Luke watched as Connie put a hand over her mouth and ran to the bathroom. The awful sounds made Luke push his plate away. He looked at Meg with eyebrows raised.

"It's okay Luke, she's fine."

They heard more noises and Luke frowned.

"Nothing to worry about. I'll pop into a chemist this morning and get something for her."

That something would be a pregnancy test.

"Do you know what Meg?" Connie handed her a wet plate to dry.

"What?"

"I'd like to be like you — you know — when I grow older."

Meg laughed. "Really? Like me?"

"No, I'm serious. You're amazing. It's like all the stuff you do here — how you've got this property running so we have a nearly normal life."

"Thanks for saying that, but really — I just had no

choice."

"Yeah, but — like — you do this thing. When you've got a problem and you don't know what to do, you really become sorta focused and you find a way around it. You never give up. I think that's just awesome."

Meg had recently noticed Connie imitating her — it was some sort of hero worship. It irritated Meg at first but then she remembered how she had done something similar when she became Angela's P.A.

It was the little things first — habits, mannerisms and particular turns-of-phrase. Angela wore jewellery that Meg admired and she found herself adopting a similar look. There was a brand of clothing that Angela preferred for every-day wear because it was functional, practical and easy to wear. Meg purchased a few items herself but was too embarrassed to wear them to work.

This stage lasted for six months or so. As she became more confident in herself and her ability, her hero-worship of Angela almost disappeared. Connie just needed to find her own strengths.

"You're awesome too. Look at how you've taken to the cooking and housework. You're so much better at it than me."

"Yeah, but that's not like the big, important stuff that

you do."

"It most certainly is! You are the engine that keeps Luke and me running so we can do all the heavy work. It's perfect now you have the baby coming. Oh, that reminds me — later I'd like to listen to the heartbeat with that special stethoscope I got from the hospital."

Connie's face fell. "Why? Do you think something's wrong?"

"Oh, sweetheart. No. Nothing at all. I think it's all more than right. I think you're having twins."

Meg dropped heavily into the chair in her bedroom and opened her journal.

"Now I'm glad I kept this written record, because not only has it helped me to work through problems but it also kept track of the days. How else would we have known that the twins were born on July 11th 2014?

Yes, today the population of our little community went from three to five. Brave Connie gave birth to one of each — a boy and a girl — both seemingly healthy although perhaps a bit underweight.

Connie is now asleep, exhausted by the protracted labour. I'm watching the proud father hovering over the babies who are also exhausted — recovering from their journey into the world. Luke's expression reflects both pride and awe.

Those two, Connie and Luke have been surprising me with their maturity and balanced view of this strange world we've found ourselves inhabiting. Connie's pregnancy was a team effort on their part, with Luke ensuring that the mother-to-be had a balanced diet and exercise plan, as well as just being there to rub oil into her distended abdomen. Often, at the end of a busy day, I'd come across them in a position that made me smile. Connie would be on the sofa, lying against a cushion with her feet in Luke's lap. Luke would be massaging her feet with a serious expression on his face. Just marvellous.

Around halfway through her pregnancy, Connie asked me to teach her to knit. Knit? I barely knew how to do it myself. Nevertheless we found a shop which stocked all the necessary supplies and we worked it out. She liked to sing while she knitted, joyful songs that made us smile. Her labours resulted in tiny cardigans and booties in a myriad of pastel shades. Each item seemed like a miracle.

As a midwife I was not qualified, competent or confident, and to me this seemed like a dangerous combination where the birth of twins was concerned. I read every book I could find on the subject and would often wake in the middle of the night, running various scenarios through my mind. I often doubted that, in the event of complications, I would be able to bring two live babies into the world.

Luck was on our side. Or perhaps that strange puppeteer who oversaw our every action had a hand in it. Connie's waters broke last

night and she progressed quickly through the stages of labour —
although I must say that it seemed like an eternity — until the first head
crowned in the early hours of the morning. This was the girl who began
making very loud noises on drawing her first breath.

The boy came not long after. He wasn't as lively as the girl. In
fact I was quite worried when he took ages to begin breathing. I gave him
a swift slap on the bottom which seemed to shock him into action. I felt
bad about that and as soon as possible, passed him to Connie for a
cuddle.

The afterbirth arrived on schedule and Luke went to bury it in
a place we'd already prepared. I'm not sure about the reason for this,
only that it seemed right — like an ancient ritual.

Now I feel the need to record these births somewhere.
Somewhere official. It must be important to humankind that Maisie
and Thomas have come into the world. Is it possible that others are being
born somewhere? Or is it just them?

What happens when they are ready to mate? Where will they
find suitable partners — or any partners for that matter?

Should Luke and I have children to widen the gene pool? I
could possibly squeeze another pregnancy or two in the time before
menopause. We wouldn't have to actually have sex — I believe a lot can
be achieved with a turkey baster. Heavens, what a thought! I laugh when
I imagine the horrified look that this suggestion would bring to Luke's
face. In any case, I'm an extremely bad candidate for a healthy

incubation of foetuses. I'll give that idea a big miss.

Tonight I'm very emotional. Seeing Luke and Connie's joy at their new babies reminds me of the loss of my own children, but at the same time I feel proud of a job well done, and this is also coloured with great relief. It's over and everyone is fine. Phew.

Now I will rack my brains to think up an idea for recording these births. History was made today."

Meg's eyes began closing of their own accord. She stirred and listened for sounds of fretful babies, and when she didn't hear any, climbed into bed. She'd need all the rest she could get.

By the time the twins were four months old, Meg had come to the heartbreaking conclusion that there was something wrong with Thomas.

She'd searched through all the medical books and the best explanation she could come up with was the term 'failure to thrive', which, like many medical terms, described the condition but not the cure.

Where Maisie was bouncing and bright and had double-chins and rolls of fat, Thomas was pale, thin and listless. He slept more than was usual and was irritable and fractious.

The three adults would spend their evenings poring over medical books, discussing plans for treatment. Many remedies were tried, but none made any difference.

If Thomas were an only child, perhaps they wouldn't have realised just how bad the situation was, but when they compared him to his incredibly bright and healthy sister, the difference was heartbreaking.

Meg felt, rightly or wrongly, that she was the custodian of the babies and their parents. One theory she had was that she was saved in order to carry out this important duty. If Thomas were to die, her sense of failure would be enormous.

"What I wouldn't give for the internet right now! I could search forums and blogs where similar symptoms were discussed by parents. I would be able to discover what treatments worked. Right now I am flying blind and I think we're losing the fight.

It is late afternoon on a day that seems almost perfect. The macadamia trees are casting lollipop shadows onto the lush grass. At this time of day, the air echoes with small noises. I can hear the cow chewing its cud. One of the lambs, born in the middle of spring, bleats at its mother. Connie sings as she washes Thomas. It's magical.

Maisie sits at my feet in a basket. She watches her fingers closely as they curl and uncurl. Her legs work constantly, using movements like a mad cyclist. She makes tiny gurgling sounds which seem to amuse her.

If only we didn't have to worry about Thomas, life would be perfect."

CHAPTER TWELVE

Meg stood watching Luke pat down the last of the loose earth with a shovel, a grim look on his face. She had helped dig the three graves — damned hard work, especially in the heavy rain— and after the bodies were placed in them, she also helped replace the earth.

While Luke put away the shovels, she made a cup of coffee and took it, and her journal, into the privacy of her bedroom. She felt the need to record the events of the past twenty four hours; in much the same way as the captain would make entries into the ship's log. Somehow it seemed important.

As she began writing, the words wouldn't flow. Too many of them raced into her brain and they bumped and tripped over each other in an attempt to be first on the page. She shifted in the chair and took a sip of coffee before again applying the pen to the paper.

"I just re-read my last entry. It was ten days ago and the world was a peaceful place. Yesterday that all changed.

For a day or so I'd felt that feeling on the back of my neck again — that sensation that I was being watched. This time I knew to trust it, so grabbed the rifle and went looking in the bush. There was nothing to see.

This feeling unsettled me and my nerves were on full alert. I kept the .22 and plenty of spare rounds close by. Connie asked me if something was wrong, but I said no — I didn't know what to tell her.

It was around mid-afternoon yesterday when I sensed a change in the air. The animals were making unusual sounds, especially the chickens that were squawking and flapping madly.

I looked outside and saw two men walking up the driveway. They walked close to each other, talking excitedly and pointing to various features of the property. Each of them was carrying a shotgun loosely by their sides.

I'm a person who doesn't like to judge people too quickly, but in the case of these two, I felt an instant dislike. No that's not right, it was distrust— a sensation that crawled over my skin like a huntsman spider, making me shiver.

I met them halfway down the driveway, my right hand holding the rifle while the left elbow supported the barrel.

They looked alike. Both wore jeans, singlets, checked

flannelette shirts and baseball caps. Both wore scruffy beards and walked with swaggers. I wondered, as they approached me, if they were related. This would be interesting in terms of scientific curiosity, that siblings had survived whatever killed the others off.

The man on my left spoke first. 'Hey, lovely lady. Nice place you 'ave 'ere.'

I nodded. 'Thanks, we like it.'

'We decided to make a friendly visit, like.' This was the man to the right. 'Perhaps you'll give us a feed and put us up for a few nights?'

My heart was beating so hard it was a wonder they couldn't hear it. My senses were heightened and time seemed to have slowed.

I sensed Luke walking up behind me. One of the children was crying in the house. A fly landed on my arm.

'Well, fellas, it's like this. It's great to see that there were more survivors, and it's nice to have met you. We're really busy at the moment, though and I wouldn't have time to be hospitable. There are lots of properties around here similar to this with sturdy houses and food available. Why don't you go and settle into one and we'll catch up soon?"

Both men smirked at the same time. This obviously wasn't what they had in mind.

'Well, that's not very friendly of 'er, is it Jimmy? Here we was thinkin' that two females would be hankerin' after a couple of lusty gents like us, if you know what I mean.' He thrust his pelvis forward and

licked his lips.

Here was a situation that life had not prepared me for. It wasn't long ago I was a housewife with a successful husband. I had been sheltered from men like these who were ill-mannered, badly educated and whose attitude suggested they could be violent. They also knew, somehow, that there were two women in the house.

I guessed that any show of weakness on my part would be pounced on. These men acted like bullies and that's what bullies do — play on weaknesses. I had to be strong, even if I was just pretending.

"Gee, that's a tempting offer, guys, but I think we'll pass."

The one to my right raised his shotgun and aimed at my legs.

"How's 'bouts you give that a bit more thought, eh?"

I felt Luke move. I shifted my left hand in an action which told him to hold firm.

"No, and I don't want any trouble. How about you two just move on and leave us alone?"

A shrill sound came from the house. It was Connie and she was screaming at the top of her lungs, "Leave us alone!" Then she screamed some more. I kept my eyes on the two men but was aware of Luke running toward the house.

The man on the left made a lunge for me, but I was ready. Any hesitation I might have felt to shoot another person was countered by Connie's screams. I lifted the rifle and shot him in the knee. The second man moved so I shot him as well, and he doubled over, clutching his abdomen. *Despite the injury to his knee, the one on the left pointed the gun at my chest so I aimed at his head and pulled the trigger. I did the same for his partner.*

Looking back I don't know how I did that. Where did the strength come from? I remember coolly examining their bodies for any sign of life and when I was certain they couldn't harm us any more, I moved on to the house.

It wasn't hard to locate the trouble. There were screams and strange male voices coming from the living area. I flattened myself against the wall of the house and made my way along the veranda. When I came to the living room window, I crouched low and looked in.

There were two men, but I only had a full view of one. He looked a lot like the two I'd just dispatched, both in appearance and manner. He was touching Connie's hair and she was being very vocal in her rejection of him, which had, luckily, drowned out the sounds of gunfire.

The fourth man had his back to me and was jiggling his whole body up and down. This seemed strange until I realised why. He had one of the babies and was calming it with movement. He seemed different to the rest, from the back anyway. He seemed better dressed and groomed.

Luke was standing in the middle of the living area, his anger evident in the tendons of his neck and the tightness of his jaw. I was concerned he was about to do something that would endanger Connie and the babies.

"So this 'ere is your man, eh? Boy is more like it. I bet I could teach ya things he's never 'eard of."

Luke seemed set to lunge forward, but then saw me signal from outside. I showed him the rifle and mouthed 'diversion'. He nodded almost imperceptibly and then closed his eyes and took a deep breath. An awful sound filled the air.

Later I found out that Luke had been a student of martial arts and that what he'd just let out was a ki-yup which is like a battle cry. It helps draw energy into the body and creates a diversion to upset the opponent. In this case his ki-yup was primal. It came from the depths of his being and through a voice that hadn't been used for a long time. It was loud, harsh and frightening.

It caused everyone in the room to turn to him in amazement. Even Connie became silent and just stared. It gave me the opportunity to slip through the sliding glass door, staying low, and to aim the rifle. The scruffy man who resembled the other two looked at me for a second with dawning comprehension. I felled him with a single bullet, but still pumped two more into him for good measure. Then I turned to the last man.

He had Thomas against his chest, but held one arm up in the universal sign of surrender.

I could see the difference in him immediately. Although his face bore a couple of day's growth, it was obvious that he shaved from time to time. He had finer features than the other three, and his eyes were clear and intelligent.

Despite the fact I'd just shot three men, I didn't want to keep killing. I wanted to find out more about this man before doing more harm. Besides, he was holding the baby.

"Connie, take Thomas from this man."

She moved forward with her arms outstretched. The man handed the child over without hesitation. I noticed that Thomas began fretting in Connie's arms, whereas he'd been unusually calm while being held by the stranger.

The man raised his other arm into the air. "I wasn't really with those other men and I want to apologise. My name is Derek."

"Luke, check him for weapons, would you?" The worst thing he was carrying was a Swiss army knife. "Now you have two whole minutes to persuade me to let you go."

I saw a quick tightening of his lips that seemed to indicate humour.

"I'll tell you my story first, but I'd appreciate if you'd lower that rifle. The way your hands are shaking is making me nervous."

He was right. I thought I'd been super-cool and controlled the whole time, but obviously not. I gave a snort of laughter, but still aimed the .22 in his direction. "Tell me your story first."

"Okay, well, I was travelling alone, but those three guys began trailing me a few days ago. They asked where I was headed and when I said Maleny, they asked to join me. We were all on foot - getting fuel

had become too hard. I mean those three guys were just drunken louts, but I felt like company after so long. They were the first live people I'd seen in what, a year and a half?"

I nodded.

"When we arrived here, I was just going to walk up the driveway, but the guys insisted it would be safer to watch the house for a day first. I didn't realise they were doing it to plan an attack. My only crime was to lead these guys to your door. That was a big one, I know, but you have to understand that I didn't expect anyone to be here."

"But, how did you find us? I don't believe for one minute that you stumbled across us accidentally."

"No, I didn't. You're going to find this hard to believe — I know it sounds ludicrous — but I was having dreams that led me here."

I saw Luke and Connie nod. Their bodies relaxed.

"Did the other three dream about this place?"

"No. Just me."

"So why were you holding Thomas? It seemed like a threat to harm him."

"No, but I can see why you'd think that. I was actually trying to protect him. His crying was upsetting Frank there." He nodded to the body on the floor. "He's such a loose cannon that I thought he might kill him to stop the noise."

"Who did you lose? Who were the people closest to you that died on May 13th?"

I saw his Adam's apple rise and fall as he swallowed hard.

"My wife and two children. My son was about the same age as that boy there."

I chewed my lip.

"Do you swear on the souls of your wife and children that you didn't intend to harm us and that you won't in the future?"

He nodded. "I swear."

I lowered the rifle. "Okay, well let's all sit down and have a coffee and you can tell us what you know."

The sky was darkening by the time Derek told us all he knew, which wasn't much more than what we had already worked out ourselves. I asked that he and Luke move the three bodies to the edge of the cleared area for burial in the morning. I prepared some dinner while Connie bathed the babies. Derek insisted on helping me in the kitchen despite my efforts to keep him out.

"No, let me help. I wanted to talk to you alone anyway."

"Oh?" I felt my body stiffen.

"No, relax. It's about Thomas. I think he needs medical attention."

"Are you a doctor?"

"Actually I'm a paediatrician. How old is Thomas now?"

A paediatrician? Wow.

"He's a little over four months. We've been worried about him."

"With good reason. If you like I'll examine him tomorrow."

I smiled at him and got the same in return. I was beginning to like this guy.

Derek was asleep on the sofa when I came out of the bedroom this morning. His long legs were hanging over the end, and his head was jammed up against the wall.

I looked over the property and saw Luke carrying shovels toward the bodies near the bush. I hurried to help him — feeling I should since I was the one who killed the men.

They were brothers, Derek told us last night, but he'd never found out their stories. He hadn't asked them for fear they'd want to hear his story and he didn't want to discuss his family with them.

Digging the graves was hard work and I was glad to be able to roll the bodies into the holes. As I threw soil over the men, I wondered about the reason they were spared on May 13th. They were such wastes of space. Worse than that, they seemed evil."

Meg stopped writing and let her mind drift over the possibilities, but couldn't understand the logic.

She thought about what she'd heard the night before — a male voice coming from Luke and Connie's room — and wondered about it. Had that diversionary cry unlocked something in Luke? Could he talk now? Why wasn't he talking to Meg then? Was he too shy?

She thought about the jobs she planned to do. Many

could be delayed until the next day. She decided then and there that, after Derek inspected Thomas, they should go for a picnic at the dam.

She made another decision. Before that she would shower thoroughly, wash her hair and shave her legs and armpits. Then she'd put on a nice dress and even perhaps make-up and perfume. She wanted to look nice for the picnic.

The day didn't go as planned, no picnic or fun — just more heartache and stress.

Derek's inspection of Thomas appeared casual so as not to worry his parents. While Luke was busy outside and Connie was doing the ironing in another room, Meg carried Thomas into the living room and placed him in Derek's arms.

The child was fretful, so the paediatrician just began his examination by holding him to his chest and murmuring softly to him. Meg could see Thomas' whole body relax and it was only then that Derek lay him down and began his examination.

At one point he put his head to Thomas' chest, his ear close to the heart. "I really need a stethoscope. I don't suppose you have one anywhere?"

"Just one of those special ones to listen to babies in the womb. Will that help?"

"No. I'll need a normal one. Any ideas?"

"Sure. I broke into a doctor's surgery not long after we came here. I could go back and look for one. Do you think it's his heart?"

"Could be but it's hard to tell. I think there's a bit of a murmur there." He re-buttoned the child's shirt. "I think we should take him to the surgery so I can examine him properly. Can you see a problem with that?"

Meg thought for a minute and went to see Connie. "Hey, Derek and I are going for a drive. We'll take Thomas for an outing."

"No need. He can just stay here with Maisie and me."

"I'd like to take him — might perk him up a bit. We won't be long."

"Oh, okay then."

Derek held Thomas tightly to his chest as he climbed into the passenger seat of the four-wheel-drive. Meg drove carefully into the township, avoiding any sharp turns or bumps. When they arrived at the doctor's surgery she parked as close to the entry as she could.

The hard work of breaking the lock had been done on her previous visit, so Meg just opened the door and held it until Derek and Thomas had passed. The examination room was cold, and she shivered.

Derek kept holding Thomas while he searched for what he needed. Once he had the instruments lined up, he lay the baby down on the examination table and gently removed his clothing.

Meg noticed that the paediatrician's hands were elegant and long-fingered. She wondered if he'd ever played the piano. He used them gracefully, and she could see he was adept at undoing the fiddly small closures of babies' clothing.

Derek warmed the stethoscope before applying it to Thomas' tiny chest. He frowned as he moved the instrument around the small area. Next he evaluated the child's reflexes and performed other tests.

He looked at Meg. "Hold him for a moment, would you? I'm going to see if I can find a portable ECG machine that runs on battery power." She could hear cupboards opening and closing for several minutes. "Ah, here we go."

He undid a plastic case and removed the machine. "Okay, now I need to stick these sensors to his chest. I have to apply this gel first and it's probably going to be cold on the poor little fellow." Thomas began whimpering as this was applied to parts of his chest. Derek moved swiftly, talking to the child in soothing tones and soon had the machine recording the electrical activity of Thomas' heart.

"We have to leave it on for around five minutes to

get any sort of idea."

Meg began roaming around the room, looking for useful medical equipment to take home. "I think you have an idea of what's wrong with him."

"Hmmm? Well, yes. I'm fairly certain it's a ventricular septal defect."

The blood drained from Meg's face. "Oh, God. That sounds terrible."

"Well, not necessarily. You've heard about kids with holes in their hearts?" Meg nodded. "Well, that's what this is. The trick is to work out how bad it is and then decide on treatment, if any."

"What do you mean, 'if any'? Why wouldn't you treat it?"

"Because if it's not large — the hole — it may heal itself in time."

"Great. But a bigger one?"

"That would usually require surgery. Sometimes it can be performed through catheters, but mostly it's a job for open-heart surgery."

"So all we need is a paediatric heart surgeon, then eh?"

Derek snorted. "Yeah, and I don't think one of those is going to come walking up your driveway."

He looked at the ECG readings. "Alrighty. That's fairly conclusive. What we need now is an x-ray and echocardiogram. There's probably a medical imaging business on the Coast here somewhere. They'll have the machines."

"So, you know how to use them?"

"Good point. Not exactly, but I could certainly give the echocardiogram a go. It's only an ultrasound machine so can't do any harm."

"So, say we do these tests and they show a large defect. What could we do?"

He shrugged.

"So what's the point? We can't operate. We can only hope it heals itself."

"True."

"Also the machines would need electricity."

Derek slapped his forehead. "Damn. Of course."

"Can drugs help?"

"Yeah, but I'll need to read up on them. Usually it would be a case of beta-blockers for heartbeat regularity, digoxin for strengthening the contractions and diuretics to reduce the volume of blood."

"That's quite a cocktail."

"Yeah, but he mightn't need all of them. That's where some proper information about the size of the hole would have come in handy."

"And I guess dosage is key in a tiny one like him?"

"Absolutely. That's why I'll have to read up on it. What I'd give for half an hour on the internet!"

"One of my new talents is finding information in books. We'll track them down in no time."

As Meg watched the stricken faces of Luke and Connie, she realised how hard the job of paediatrician must be in those cases where the child has problems.

Derek had been very gentle and patient with them, letting each fact register before moving on to the next.

"I guess we always knew there was something wrong — but his heart? That's awful!" Tears were spilling onto Connie's hands that were clenched in her lap.

"What we need to do is make sure he gets plenty of the right nutrients. He doesn't feed well because he becomes breathless and tires, so we have to find a way to get around this. The stronger he is, the better he can fight the problem and perhaps heal it himself. I'll have to do some reading and formulate a plan."

Luke and Connie nodded.

"I'm also researching drugs that can help. I'll know more in a couple of days."

"Anything we can do in the meantime?"

"Definitely. He needs to be held a lot. I've already been doing this. It keeps him quiet and lowers his stress levels."

Meg leaned back in her chair and crossed her legs. "I've noticed that. He relaxes, especially when you hold him."

"I've had lots of practice. What I suggest is that we all take turns, the more the better."

Meg smiled at this man who only two days ago was the enemy. Now he was volunteering for baby holding.

Derek took Connie's hand. "You must realise that this is a common defect and with careful handling it won't cause any major concerns."

Only if the hole isn't too big, thought Meg.

CHAPTER THIRTEEN

"Aw, c'mon. How do you know all this stuff?" Meg was leaning on her shovel, looking at Derek who had just come up with a solution for fencing that took her breath away.

"What stuff?"

"Knowledge just seems to flow out of you. How to do things and fix things. It's unbelievable!"

He frowned.

"Like that fencing thing. You just knew that. Have you ever fenced a property in your life?"

"No, but, well, it's just common sense."

"Common sense, eh? How about that tool you fixed last week? You took it into the shed for fifteen minutes and when you brought it out again it looked brand new."

"It really wasn't hard."

"No, not hard because you have this ... this font of knowledge inside you."

His eyes crinkled at the edges. "Font of knowledge?"

"And direction. You always know what direction you're facing, wherever you are you just — know."

"It's a guy thing."

"Well, I think it's bloody unfair that you have this 'guy thing' and I don't. Here we are, trying to survive in this world that's messed up and you have a whole set of skills I don't."

"That's not right. You know all sorts of things I don't."

"Like what?"

"You know. Sewing and knitting..."

"I actually don't know much about that."

"Cooking?"

"You cook just as well as me. That Asian dish you served last night was amazing."

"Fluke."

"Rubbish."

He smiled.

"Anyway, I still say it's unfair. Oh, and by the way, we should work out a better place for you to sleep."

"Why?"

"I know the sofa isn't very comfortable."

He shrugged. "It's okay."

"I can hear you tossing and turning from my room. We can sort something better."

Or you could just slip into my bed— bring that gorgeous body of yours and hold it against mine. We would fit together just nicely, I assure you. You'd slide inside me like a hand into a glove and I'd be ready for you. You'd start to move gently...

"It's not just the sofa. I don't sleep well."

"Oh?"

"Haven't done for a long time." He looked away.

"Well the offer's there. I know there aren't any bedrooms left, but I slept in that cosy little shed when I first arrived and it was nice. There's already furniture in there. Or we could tow a caravan here..."

"No need. I'll probably be moving on soon anyway."

Meg felt like a bucket of cold water had been poured over her. "Oh, I didn't know...I thought..." She ran out of words.

"I wanted to stay until Thomas stabilised. He's improved a great deal and the medication seems spot on. There's not much more I can do."

"But where will you go?"

"Dunno."

"You know you are more than welcome to stay. I guess we've never actually told you that."

"Thanks, it's appreciated. It's just..."

"What?"

"This is such a cosy family situation. I don't belong."

"They're not my family. I don't really belong either. I'm guessing they'll move to their own place soon."

"But still..."

"This is all just rubbish. You belong here just as much as the rest of us."

"Meg. I had a family. The best family a man could want. I just..." He took a shuddering breath. "I just can't..." He threw down his shovel and walked into the bush.

He didn't return until dinner time, and then he averted his gaze from Meg's.

Meg had trouble sleeping. Derek's words kept rolling like waves through her mind. Eventually she gave up and reached for her journal.

"Is it so far-fetched that Derek and I might have got together? We're around the same age, fit, healthy, and heterosexual. It's like the old song, "If you were the only girl in the world..."

It seems I am the only available girl in the world and still he rejects me. How bad is that? What's wrong with me?

He seems like a good man. Is that the problem? Is it only the bastards that are attracted to me? I mean, really...

My body is good — well as good as it gets for someone with my build. I have just the one scar from the caesareans and Derek's never seen it. I'm not sagging anywhere and there's no excess fat at all. My face is good — perhaps showing some sun damage but it makes me look healthy. My features are regular. I've got hazel eyes and a wide mouth. My hair is okay now — short but with the corkscrew curls I've always had. It's a dark-blonde colour, but the sun has been streaking it a bit. Overall I reckon I'm okay. I certainly don't think I'd repulse a man like Derek.

I wonder what his wife was like. Connie asked about her once and he said she'd been a paediatric anaesthetist. British.

Is it her? Is she haunting him? Is he feeling guilty for surviving when they all died? Or maybe he is still in love with her and can't be with anyone else. Maybe.

I remember a conversation we had one night. I'd been out getting supplies for dinner and on impulse stopped at a bottle shop for wine. We were having fish from Baroon Pocket Dam, so I got the best Sauvignon Blanc I could find — from Marlborough New Zealand.

I dished out the meals and handed them around to everyone at the table. Then I brought over the wine and two glasses. When I went to pour some for him, he shook his head and covered the glass. I just sipped mine throughout the meal.

Afterwards he came to help with the dishes and saw me pouring the rest of the wine down the sink.

"Seems a waste. Sorry about that. I had a bad experience with alcohol after...you know..."

I laughed. "Me too. A whole bottle of vodka in one night. Not good."

His smile was ironic. "A big single night of drinking would have been perfect. Mine was a big year. Really messed myself up."

"Oh, I'm sorry."

"I finally decided to dry out. It was hard to do and I swore off the booze."

"Sure. I understand."

"In all that time I was drinking, I hardly moved from where our house was."

"Where was that?"

"Coogee in Sydney. I was living like a tramp. I eventually realised that I had to start moving. I picked north."

"Then you started having dreams?"

"A couple of months later. I'd been taking my time moving up the coast, staying a while in each town. When the dreams became more persistent, I moved more quickly."

"So you were on foot, even in those early stages?"

He laughed. "Yeah, well I started in a car, but without a plan for when I ran out of gas. I thought I'd syphon some — nothing worked. I'd swap cars, but the unlocked ones had dead people in them. I wasn't like you with your great pump solution — that was a stroke of genius by the way. I think my brain was still recovering from the alcohol abuse and I couldn't think very clearly. Anyway, I just began walking and that suited me."

"It doesn't help, does it...the booze I mean."

"No, it doesn't. But then, nothing does."

Now when I think of those words I realise that he is still battling some demons. There is probably no way I can fight these."

As she closed the book, she did so with a feeling of acceptance.

Meg told Connie what Derek was planning and saw the shock show on Connie's face. "No! What about Thomas? We need him here!"

"I know. He's been so good to all of us, but he wants to move on. He's restless. I believe he's still in shock over losing his family."

"We all lost family."

"It was different for him. He lost a spouse and two children. I think he loved his wife a great deal. It's hell to have children die, but to lose a loving and supportive wife at the same time? I think he's a very sensitive man and he just can't move on from that — not now anyway."

"I sorta thought that you and him..."

"Yeah, me too."

"Did you try?"

"Try what?"

"You know, come on to him."

"No, Connie. I've never 'come on' to any man."

"What, they've just fallen at your feet?"

Meg laughed. "I've only had two men in my life. Both showed interest in me first and then I showed interest back. I don't like to be, you know, aggressive. I wait until I'm asked."

"And you've never got signals from Derek?"

"Not a one."

"But if you did come on to him a bit and it worked, then he might stay. Could be worth a try."

"Or he'd reject me, and it would be awkward, and he'd go away sooner, which I think would be the more likely outcome."

"It's not fair. I want him to stay!"

"So do I, believe me, but we have to play this smart. If we make it easy for him to go, he might be more inclined to return if he sorts himself out. What do you think?"

"Yeah, I guess so."

"So, we'll make that our game plan, then?"

"Okay, I'll let Luke know."

"That's what I've been meaning to ask you. Is Luke talking to you?"

"Sometimes. Not much."

"Still, it's a good sign."

Despite the sensible attitude she adopted when talking to Connie, Meg still plotted to delay Derek's departure. The fencing job — to enclose the entire property — was almost completed, and she wondered if he planned to leave after that.

She racked her brains to think of projects he'd find interesting or fulfilling. Then she thought she should plan some that were clearly beyond her capacity. She left drawings and notes around the house, hoping he'd find them and stay to help do them.

She loved watching him work. His tall, lean frame moved easily. However, sometimes she saw him wince and rub the small of his back as he straightened, but he never complained of any ailments.

Derek's moods were clear to Meg when she looked at his eyes. She could tell when his demons were chasing him, and she'd leave him alone, waiting for the return of the clear, bright humour that shone from him when everything was good.

"I wonder how long he will suffer and if he will ever fully recover. Will any of us? I think it's a case of just moving forward — not dwelling on horrors that cloud the spirit and rot the soul."

The morning after the fence was completed, Meg found two letters on the dining table, one marked "to Luke and Connie", while the other just said "Meg."

She didn't have to read her note to know he'd gone — she could already feel his absence in the air. She unfolded it slowly.

"Meg. I don't think you know how hard it has been for me to be around you. I have felt your need for me — you wanted me to be your man — but I just can't be that person.

I feel I've done my duty. I owed you for bringing those low-lifes to your door. Do you know how magnificent you were that day when you shot them? You did the human race a huge favour by dispatching them so efficiently. Just imagine how much havoc their genes would have caused in this limited gene-pool?

In any case, Thomas no longer needs constant monitoring and I've left a note with detailed instructions for Luke and Connie. These will help him into the future. We can only hope the condition heals itself.

We have finished the fence at last. I know there are more jobs yet, and I know you could really use my help, but I must go. Sadly.

My plan is to go down to the coast and just hang out there for a while. Maybe I'll move a bit further north. I'd like to think that I'd be welcome to return one day, even if it's just to check on Thomas' condition. He's the only patient I have in the world so I shouldn't neglect him.

You'll do great in the future. I've often admired your can-do attitude and no-fuss approach. You think I have an advantage over you — some secret inbuilt knowledge, but I don't have your drive and determination, without which my knowledge is useless. I could never have achieved what you have on that property.

You shot those men seemingly easily and then later showed a vulnerability that made me want to hold you. You're very special and I will never forget the time I've spent with you. D x"

This letter acted like a magic potion to Meg. There were no words of love but he had taken the time to describe his admiration for her.

Although she felt his absence like an open sore, his note had given her the gift of hope that one day he would return.

CHAPTER FOURTEEN

Meg was in the chicken coop collecting eggs when she heard a sound so unbelievable that she dropped the three she had collected and ran to where she had a clear view of the sky.

Connie ran from the house, rubbing her hands on a tea towel. Luke came from the machinery shed. They grouped together and watched the sky until Connie squealed, "There it is!"

It was a black helicopter, and it came toward them unsteadily and hovered over the house. Meg realised she'd left the coop open and the chickens were running crazily over the lawn, frightened by the sound. The animals in the enclosure were round-eyed with fear. Meg was frightened and exhilarated. What did this mean?

She could see a figure in the cockpit, fighting with

the controls. She waved and pointed to the end of the property where there was room to land. Eventually the aircraft moved and landed where she wanted.

The door to the cockpit opened. The pilot undid his harness and disembarked. The first thing she noticed was his strange gait. He walked awkwardly, like he was all loose inside.

He was dressed in a black suit, white shirt and thin black tie. Although it seemed he was well-dressed, the outfit didn't work properly. The suit seemed badly-cut or wrong for his body.

He was swarthy with wavy black hair — a bit greasy — and brown eyes. As he moved toward them Meg noticed that Luke and Connie took a step back so they were behind her.

"Hello there." She kept her tone light. "Where have you come from?"

He shook his head and handed her a piece of paper. As she took it she noted it was just as standard A4 sheet. The printing said:

WE HAVE COME TO HELP YOU WITH MEDICAL MATTERS, INCLUDING THE BOY'S HEART. ALL OF YOU PLEASE PACK A SMALL SUITCASE

CONTAINING ONLY ESSENTIALS TO LAST FOR A FEW DAYS. YOU WILL BE TRANSFERED BY HELICOPTER.

Meg raised her eyebrows and shook the letter at the man. "But who is this from? Where would you take us? You don't just expect us to pack up and go away without knowing more?"

The man just raised his hands and shook his head. Connie stepped forward and whispered in her ear. "I don't think he understands you."

"Well, what about the animals? Who's going to look after them? I should stay behind."

"Oh, no. Please don't. We might need you."

"Luke, what do you think? Should we go?" He nodded.

Connie nodded too. "Luke would say yes because they talk about Thomas' heart. I say yes too. They know about it. Do you think Derek sent these people?"

"No, he would have come himself."

Meg turned to the pilot. "Are you sure we'll only be gone a few days?" He raised his hands helplessly. Then he pointed to his watch.

"Okay, we'll come." Connie had already begun

walking toward the house. Luke ran to catch up and put his arm around her shoulders in a protective gesture. She was pregnant again — they'd only just confirmed it that morning. Meg wondered what was going through their minds.

She looked at the man again, trying to work it all out. He just stared back. After a few seconds he tapped his watch and she went inside the house to pack.

Meg realised that her selection of items to pack would seem strange. She started with her journal, fountain pen and refills and then added the book by the Vietnamese Zen Monk. Another book, about survival tips, was added to the pile. Her army knife and multi-tool came next and it was only after all those things were stowed in pockets of her backpack that she began thinking about clothing and toiletries.

After doing up the clasps of the backpack, she went into the spare bedroom to see if she could help Connie pack for the twins. They had everything under control so she moved outside and handed the backpack to the pilot. She returned all the chickens to the coop and made sure they had plenty of food and water. By the time she'd finished attending to the other animals, the rotors of the helicopter had begun turning.

Luke, Connie and the twins came out of the house,

the children looking at the helicopter with wide eyes. There weren't enough seats for all of them, so the twins sat on Luke and Connie's laps.

As the helicopter rose unsteadily over the property, Meg looked down and was able to see what they had achieved in the time they had lived there. She felt proud and also anxious about leaving it.

The helicopter ride was thankfully short, just to Maroochy Airport where a small jet was waiting. Meg could see a pilot in the cockpit and noticed that he seemed similar to the man who flew the helicopter, who was bringing up the rear. He was carrying their luggage and kept dropping items. He seemed frustrated at his lack of co-ordination.

As Meg walked up the steps to the jet, she looked around her carefully. She wondered about other people — who was in the control tower? Who was re-fuelling aircraft? The airport seemed totally deserted.

The helicopter pilot joined the other man in the cockpit and the jet engines were started. After a short taxi they were airborne.

"What do you think of all of this, Meg? What's happening?" Connie was pale, her freckles standing out starkly from her face.

"I have no idea. I guess the best thing is to just go with the flow. Try not to worry. If they wanted to harm us, they would have done so by now."

"I just wish they'd talk to us."

"Yeah, I know. Seems they can't."

They hit some turbulence which made them fall silent. The children began whimpering. Luke and Connie tried to settle them down.

As the jet levelled out, Connie began again. "Do you think they'll keep us for long? What will they do to us?"

"Don't' know, Connie, and it's useless trying to speculate. Just wait and see."

"Oh, Christmas! It's Christmas Eve! All those plans we had. The presents for the kids..."

Meg felt a pang then. They had decided to make Christmas a big event and had been planning for weeks. Those plans were now in disarray.

"Doesn't matter, Connie. The kids won't know the difference if we celebrate it a bit later. We make up our own rules now, you see."

Meg looked out the window and noticed they were over land, not water. She could see the coast disappearing behind them which meant they were flying inland, maybe west or northwest. After some time the vegetation became sparser and she heard the engines slow. They had begun their descent.

The aircraft hit the runway with a jolt, which upset the children all over again. Meg shifted in her seat, looking out each window to see what airport they had landed at. All she could see was a shed with no signs on it. The door of the aircraft opened, and as Meg stood at the top of the steps to disembark, she noticed there was a bus waiting.

The two pilots were waiting at the bottom of the steps. Meg didn't know which was which. Not only did they look similar but they were dressed the same and both walked with that strange, disjointed gait. Were they twins?

The bus looked as though it would seat around twenty people, but they were the only passengers. The road was uneven, and they were constantly being flung from side to side. After ten minutes or so they stopped in front of a low, white building.

Just like the airport, this facility, whatever it was, bore no signage. Meg tried to take in every detail, and as they walked through the front doors, was interested to note that they were automatic — powered by electricity. Air conditioning units hummed.

They were led through an area which looked like its purpose was a reception desk, but there was no one manning it. After that was a large, red door which one of the men opened before motioning them through.

This room was like a dormitory, with three beds and a bathroom. Beside each bed was a small chest of drawers that also acted as a table. There was a metal frame on wheels next to the door which contained coat-hangers. Everything in the room was bright white.

Connie sat on one of the beds with a child on each side of her. Luke and Meg began stowing their possessions. The men moved behind Connie and took a child each and then left, closing the door behind them. It happened so suddenly that the adults had no time to react, although Meg almost made it to the door before it closed. She heard the click of a lock.

Connie's face began to crumble and Meg moved toward her. She and Luke talked to her gently, suggesting she stay calm for the good of her unborn child.

After a while, Luke tried the door. They knew what the result would be. He returned to the bed with a downturned mouth.

Meg looked outside. The sun was beating down harshly on the land around the building. She figured they were in the desert, or close to it. The vegetation was low and scrubby, the soil arid.

She turned and removed some items from the backpack. The survival book she gave to Luke. The one on Zen Buddhism was passed to Connie, in the hopes it would calm her. Meg settled onto a bed and began writing in her journal.

The sun was low in the sky when they heard the door being unlocked. Meg jumped to her feet and ran toward it, confronting one of the men as soon as it opened.

"How dare you! You can't treat us like this! You've snatched the children and locked us up like criminals. I won't have it!"

The man's eyebrows shot into his hairline. He took a step backward and held up his hands. The other man was standing behind him with a paper cup, which he handed to Meg while indicating with sign language that she should drink it.

She sniffed the contents. "What is it?" The men made the drinking motion again. "Okay, I'll do what you say, but stop locking us up. Where are the children?" Two sets of brown eyes just looked at her.

She shook her head in frustration and drank the contents of the cup in one swallow. They led her to another room and pointed to an examining table. She sat down on it and then realised she had to lie down very quickly.

When Meg woke she was alone in the room. There was a sheet covering her and she realised she was naked from the waist down. Her clothes were on a chair. As she sat up she felt the sensation in her genitals of just having had a pelvic exam, like a pap-smear. Like she'd been stretched open and she could feel there had been an application of lubricant. It wasn't an uncomfortable sensation — quite pleasurable.

She wondered what other medical tests they had run. She also wondered who had performed them. The two pilots didn't look like medicos, but there hadn't been any sign of other people in the building. The only voices they heard were their own.

Back in the dormitory she found the door unlocked, but one of the men was standing outside it. Connie looked even paler, and Meg was becoming quite concerned. She wondered briefly about attacking the men and escaping, but quickly realised they had no means of getting away. They couldn't fly a jet. Besides, the men still had the children somewhere.

Luke was led away next and came back after an hour or so, scowling. Next it was Connie's turn. Meg walked to the door with her and looked at the man taking her away. "Be gentle with her, she's pregnant." He didn't acknowledge this, and they moved away.

Luke couldn't sit still. He paced for the whole time Connie was gone, which was over an hour. When she returned, she told of being blind-folded and taken to a room where various tests were performed: blood pressure, heart, and something that felt like an ultrasound of her abdomen and womb.

Meg was beginning to feel murderous. They hadn't been fed or given water. She opened the unlocked door and looked at the man outside it. "How about some food and water?" He held up his hands. She shut the door again.

Around half an hour later the door opened again, and the men entered, bearing trays of food and drink. Meg, Connie and Luke fell on the food hungrily, but were soon pulling faces. It was barely edible. They drank the water thirstily.

After the trays were removed the three of them settled down to reading and writing. After an hour or so the lights were turned off, and eventually they fell asleep.

With daylight came another almost inedible meal, but it also brought Maisie. As she was carried through the door she caught sight of Connie and her bottom lip began to wobble. Connie leapt from the bed, ran to her and snatched her out of the arms of the man. "What about Thomas? What's happening with him?" The man just turned and left the room.

The day seemed interminable. Connie let Maisie crawl around the floor while the three adults began to boil with impotent fury.

Books were swapped and Meg tried composing haiku poems to ease the boredom. At one stage she carefully tore a page from her journal so that she and Luke could play noughts and crosses.

Darkness fell, and then the lights were turned off.

They heard Thomas before the door opened. All three adults jumped to their feet, and even Maisie began crawling toward the door.

Connie was there first to take the boy into her arms and soothe his crying. As she jiggled him and whispered in his ear, one of the men handed Meg a note:

WE WILL TRANSPORT YOU HOME.

The other was holding a device that Meg had never seen before. He stepped forward and took Luke by the arm, turning it until the soft, fleshy part of the forearm was exposed. He held the device to a place halfway to the elbow and pressed a button. Luke flinched for a second.

The man reached for Connie's arm and she frowned

but held it out. The same procedure was carried out on her.

When they moved toward Meg she took a step backward. The second man walked in and stood behind her. "Just tell me what this is. What are you doing?" She looked at Luke and he shrugged. The sooner she let them do whatever it was, the sooner they could all go home. She felt a quick bolt of pain in her arm, but then it went away.

Both men went and stood by the door. One tapped his watch, so Meg began throwing her things into a backpack. "C'mon guys. Let's get outta here. Bill and Ben here are already impatient." Luke and Connie laughed.

CHAPTER FIFTEEN

Meg had the sharpest knife she owned in her right hand and was running it along the edge of whatever was sitting under the skin of her forearm. She figured it was an implant that either kept track of her whereabouts or monitored her physical condition — maybe both. In any case, it irritated her and she was about to get rid of it.

Luke was in the living room, busy with the after Christmas dinner activities of helping the children play with their new toys. Meg could hear Connie running water into the sink, ready to wash a kitchen-full of dishes.

She steadied her right hand and pushed into the skin, making a line along the edge of the implant. She dabbed at the blood with a cloth and saw the cut needed to be deeper. After a deep breath she plunged the knife deeper into her flesh and was rewarded with the sight of the edge of the device. She removed it with tweezers.

The mystery for her was how the implant was put into her arm without leaving a wound — it would have made removal a hell of a lot easier.

After treating the cut and wrapping a dressing and bandage around it, she inspected the innocent looking piece of blue plastic. There were no words or numbers printed on it. No sign of circuits. What was it?

She shook her head and placed the device on a shelf. "That'll teach those bastards."

Walking through the living room she saw a sight that made her smile. It was Thomas, and he was crawling around madly, playing with the Christmas wrappings and crowing in delight. He saw Maisie examining a bow tied onto a ribbon and, before anyone knew what was happening, had snatched it from her and crawled off in the opposite direction. Meg and Luke looked at each other and smiled — he was actually being naughty. That was new.

In the three days since they'd arrived home from the desert, Thomas had improved dramatically. His skin colour was brighter and his energy levels had increased dramatically. Meg decided they should stop giving him the drugs Derek had prescribed, and he certainly didn't miss them.

The only evidence that he'd undergone any treatment in the strange hospital was a dressing on his leg, up near the groin. When Connie removed this, she found a tiny cut that had already mostly healed. What did they do to him? More importantly, who were '*they*'?

"Hey you guys. Come and sit down a minute. We need to talk."

The children were in bed, and a welcome peace had fallen over the house. Luke and Connie joined Meg in the lounge room.

"We haven't had time to think since we got back — all that catching up, and then making Christmas. Now we need to talk about what the hell happened with those helicopter dudes."

"What's wrong with your arm?"

Meg looked at the bandaging and then back at Connie. "I took out that implant thing."

"What? How?"

"With a knife."

"Wow. Do you think that's wise?"

"It was irritating me and I reckon it might have been some sort of tracking device. Those guys really pissed me off the way they treated us."

"Bill and Ben?" Connie thought that was very funny.

"Yeah, Bill and Ben. So, back to the question. Any ideas?"

Connie cleared her throat. "Well, I've got one idea. Those two men — you know how they looked — darkish skin and greasy hair. Perhaps they were middle-eastern. Perhaps some radical group from over there somewhere let off some sort of biological weapon, but it was stronger than they thought and it killed most people in the world. The ringleaders were protected, of course. Now they are either acting to save the human race, or are just interested in us to see why we didn't die."

Meg pursed her lips and nodded. "I guess that's as good a theory as any." She looked at Luke. "Any theories, Luke?"

He looked startled that Meg had asked him a direct question. He remained silent.

"Jeez, Luke. I know you talk sometimes. I hear your voice in the bedroom. Sometimes I need your opinions, okay?"

He looked like a rabbit trapped in the headlights of a car. He shrugged.

"Okay — well if that's the way you want it, you can write me a note or relay it through Connie. Whatever." She walked into her bedroom, closing the door firmly after her.

CHAPTER SIXTEEN

Meg was sitting on the toilet seat, staring with disbelief at the pregnancy test results. A blue line in the window. Holy crap.

All along she thought the symptoms might have been signs of early menopause. It happened to her mother, so it could easily happen to her. Then she saw the pregnancy test kits in the bathroom cupboard — the ones they had left over from Connie's test — and thought she'd at least rule pregnancy out. It didn't rule it out.

How in the hell?

"I just don't believe this. I wonder how far I'm gone. Perhaps the test is wrong, it has to be. That's it. Unless...

That exam they did on me at that hospital they took us to. I thought it was a pap-smear or something. Maybe it wasn't. What did they do? Rape me? IVF? It would be more likely the latter. Did they just implant an embryo — in which case it wouldn't be my egg? Or did they introduce sperm into my womb?

I think this is it. I think that something was done to me there that has resulted in this pregnancy. I just don't know exactly what it was.

*Now I'm **really** pissed off with these guys. What the hell do they think they're doing? How do they think they can get away with this, and to what end? Will the child be swarthy and greasy and walk weirdly?*

What's going on, damn it? Jeez, I'm going to throw up again...

I'm back. The thought of this pregnancy scares me. I didn't make a good incubator for Nicholas or Emily. In the end I had to have emergency caesareans, for their sakes as well as mine. And then there was that other baby — the night everyone died. How long ago was that? Today is May 3rd 2015 — so it was around twenty-two months ago. I wouldn't want to go through that again.

No, I don't think I want to do this. For one thing it's unwise without good medical support. For another, I really just don't know what is growing inside me.

I guess I need an abortion, but who's going to do it? No one I can think of. What were the old wives' remedies? Gin and a hot bath? Something about knitting needles? Heavens!

What was that abortion pill — the one that caused all that fuss a few years back? I have to find out. Fast.

The library provided the name of the drug — mifepristone, and the chemist had some on their shelves. Meg took the two tablets while standing in the shop and then went home to wait it out.

They worked quickly and she was left with cramping and bleeding for some time afterwards.

"I don't feel any sense of guilt or loss — just an overwhelming relief that I no longer have that thing in my body — whatever it was.

Connie and Luke took turns to sit with me through the worst of the abortion, Connie would sit and stroke my forehead and sing quietly. That was nice. She also brought me a hot water bottle which helped ease the cramps.

I got rid of that foetus within hours of finding out about it. Now it's time to take some pain killers and catch up on the jobs that have been neglected.

Oh, just one other thing. While I was researching mifepristone, I also looked up something else I'd been meaning to find out about. Thomas' condition has improved so much that he now appears like a normal child of his age. I looked up surgical procedures to treat holes in the hearts of infants, and found there is one that has been used on occasion if the situation allows. 'Cardiac catheterization' is when access to the heart is made possible by inserting a flexible tube into a blood vessel, often in the leg near the groin — just where I found that dressing on him.

I guess we should be grateful to those dribbling arseholes for that."

The next time the helicopter approached, Meg stopped still to listen and then ran to the shelf where the rifle was kept. She checked the magazine was full and put spare rounds in her pocket. By the time Bill or Ben (whichever it was) landed the helicopter unsteadily and got to the veranda, she was ready.

His eyes grew large when he saw the rifle and raised his arms. He had a note in one hand and Meg reached over and grabbed it.

THIS MAN WILL TAKE ONE OF YOU AWAY FOR MEDICAL TREATMENT.

YOU HAVE 20 MINUTES TO PACK A SUITCASE.

PLEASE CO-OPERATE.

The man pointed at Meg. She shook her head. He pointed again. She shook her head again. He tapped his watch. She raised the rife to his eye level.

He backed away and returned to the helicopter, taking off shortly after.

Connie came and stood next to Meg. "I wonder what they'll do to us now." Her voice was high and thin.

The three adults went about their work as usual, but had underlying concerns about what would happen after Meg's refusal to go with the man in the helicopter. After three days they found out. By then it seemed almost like an anti-climax, except for the surge of adrenaline it caused.

It was both Bill and Ben who approached the back veranda this time. One carried a large bag, while the other was the bearer of a new note:

THE MEN ARE HERE TO CONDUCT MEDICAL TESTS. YOU WILL NOT BE TAKEN AWAY.

PLEASE CO-OPERATE.

Meg read it twice, trying to find any hidden meaning. She decided to allow them in but told Connie to stay by her side no matter what. She had already decided to refuse any liquids out of paper cups.

They unpacked some equipment and then one of them pointed to Thomas. His test was similar to the one Meg saw Derek perform in the doctor's surgery. The men didn't look at the results, but just folded the piece of paper which indicated the electrical activity of Thomas' heart and placed it in the bag.

Next they took Luke's forearm and examined the place the implant had been inserted. Then they did the same to Connie.

Connie's blood pressure was checked. They gave her a bottle with a label that read 'urine sample' and nodded to her. She complied. Then they checked her forearm.

Bill and Ben moved over to Meg. The urine sample request came first. As she handed the full bottle to them, one of them reached out and grabbed her left arm. She heard a joint intake of breath as they realised what she had done. One of the men went out to the helicopter and returned with the machine that inserted implants. As he walked toward Meg, she looked around for the rifle, but then saw the expression on Luke's face. She looked at Connie who was shaking her head.

Meg just wanted these guys to disappear so the five of them could return to a peaceful existence, but could see that Connie and Luke were worried and wanted her to co-operate. She realised they were probably right. None of them knew exactly who they were dealing with yet and caution was prudent. She held her arm toward the man with the machine and flinched as a new device was inserted into her flesh.

As soon as the helicopter faded into the distance, however, she grabbed the sharp knife and added the second device to the other on the bathroom shelf.

CHAPTER SEVENTEEN

One morning in August, Meg woke and saw the gifts that the day was offering, and decided to take some time off to go fishing at the dam. The thought made her feel light and happy.

Before breakfast, she dug in the garden until she had ten worms wiggling in the bottom of an empty tin. She almost skipped inside and as she passed Luke, she waved the worms under his nose. "Fishing! Wanna come?"

He shook his head and cradled his arms around an imaginary distended abdomen. "Yeah absolutely, you should stay close to Connie. Those new twins are making life tough for her."

"Gawd you're not wrong there." Connie was waddling out of the bedroom, one hand on her enormous belly and the other holding her lower back. I think I'm going to burst open soon."

"Oh, what a thought! Hey, why don't you stay in bed today?"

"No, I wanna move around."

"Well you should get Luke to make you breakfast in bed at least. I'm just going to grab some coffee and fruit and I'll go and catch us some fish.

She opened the sunroof and whistled as she drove down to the dam. The boat was easy to manoeuvre into the water from the place she'd left it last time. The rods and lines were all ready to go. Soon she was rowing out to the middle.

Fish stocks had risen greatly since all the fishermen except Meg had died. It wasn't long until there were five splashing around in the bucket, but they were mostly perch, so she decided to move to another spot to try for bass.

As she was picking up the oars, she heard the horn of the tractor blasting. Luke was standing by the shore, waving his arms. Meg rowed quickly toward him, noticing he was carrying a piece of paper. He was breathing heavily.

The note was in Connie's writing. "My waters have just broken and things are happening very quickly. Please come. We need you."

Meg finished reading and looked at Luke.

"Ask me yourself."

He frowned.

"Ask me yourself, goddamn it. I'm in no mood for your silliness anymore. You're a man and a father. Ask me or you can deliver the twins yourself."

He lowered his gaze to the ground and then began walking away. Meg nearly gave in at that point.

He had gone twenty metres or so before he turned around and jogged back.

"We need you." His voice was harsh and croaky. Meg gave him a big hug.

"Jump in the car. We'll be there in minutes."

The babies were born, but amid much blood and madness.

Meg realised partway through the labour that she'd been too confident — the birth of Maisie and Thomas had gone all right, so she had approached this one with a relaxed manner. All three — Connie and her two daughters — survived, but it was touch and go. Meg felt as though she barely survived the trauma herself, while Luke was traumatised after seeing his precious Connie in such a state.

The labour seemed to go forever, and the babies were both very big. Their heads were huge. Meg had to cut Connie's perineum to allow the babies passage into the world. It was a big decision to make — doing the cutting — but she thought that if she didn't, Connie would tear and the babies would be more distressed.

At one point she thought about the Bill and Ben, thinking that she wouldn't mind if they landed their helicopter and came to help. No such luck.

From time to time Maisie or Thomas would come to the door and stare in with wide eyes. Meg would have to remind Luke to take them somewhere and entertain them.

Connie's blood loss was acute, and Meg thought she needed a transfusion. That was all beyond her. She didn't know how to test herself or Luke for compatibility. She didn't know how to go about setting up the transfusion.

After it was all over and Meg had checked the babies over, she handed one of the girls to Luke. "Remind me to talk to you about contraception. She can't do this again for at least a couple of years." She saw that he had tears in his eyes. "Also, formula. We're going to bottle-feed these two to give Connie a chance to recover."

"No way!" Connie's voice seemed to come from a long way, even though she was just beside them.

"For God's sake, Connie — be sensible! It won't matter. I'm sure the formula in the stores will still be within use-by dates. It will be easier and the babies won't be sucking the energy out of you."

"Nope. No way. Tell her Luke! We won't have our babies bottle-fed."

Luke looked from Connie to Meg and shook his head, then walked outside with his new baby daughter.

"Ha! You'd think he'd stand up for me after all this, wouldn't you?"

"Don't worry Connie. He's just too overwhelmed. If you feel that strongly about it..."

"Absolutely."

"At least you have age on your side. You'll bounce back. I insist that you take iron tablets and some special vitamins for breast-feeding mothers as well. I'll get some tomorrow."

Connie lay back on the pillow and turned her head to one side. Meg saw she had fallen asleep. She leaned over and kissed her on the forehead. "What a brave little thing you are."

CHAPTER EIGHTEEN

Meg was standing at the wall in the lounge room, looking at the needle on the barometer. She was chewing her lip.

Connie came to look at what was of so much interest. "Oh, the barometer. Dad used to have one in his study, and I'd see him looking at it sometimes, especially if he planned a long boat trip. What's up?"

"It's dropping — the barometric pressure that is — really fast. That's why it's so dark out to the east. I think we're in for some nasty weather."

"Oh? Um...you don't mean like a cyclone, do you?" She jiggled three-month-old Rosie and patted her on the back.

"You know I'm a Melbourne girl, Connie. I don't know much about cyclones. You're from Cairns, though. You must know more than me."

"I hate them. They're just so scary."

"Do they normally come down this far south? I've never heard of one hitting the Sunshine Coast with any force."

"Me neither. Isn't it too early for cyclones anyway? It's only November."

"Maybe it'll just be a severe storm then. Anyway, you're in charge."

"In charge? Of what?"

"Of storm/cyclone preparation. You've lived through them. Make a list. Educate us."

"But..."

"But what?"

"I don't know much. Mum and Dad used to take care of everything. And the babies..."

"Still — you know more than I do. Listen, Luke and I will have to go outside and secure everything we can. We'll have to put the animals somewhere safe. While we're doing that, we'll need you to be looking after stuff here. Don't we have to tape up windows or something? Store fresh water? I know you're busy with the girls, but I'll come in and help as soon as I can. "

"Um...yeah, okay."

"Great, hop to it." Meg saw Luke walking past the

house. "Oi, Luke. C'mon, I need your muscles."

By nightfall they had secured everything as best they could. Connie was struggling to reach high enough to tape some of the windows, so Luke helped. They ran out of tape before all the glass was secured, but the weather was already closing in, so there was no chance to drive anywhere to get more.

They ate a light dinner, and then sat in the living room, round-eyed, listening to the wind, which was increasing in speed rapidly.

Meg clapped her hands. "Well, there's only one thing to do on a night like this."

Connie was getting paler by the minute. "What?"

"Break out the Monopoly board of course — and play some soothing music."

"You sound just like my parents did when cyclones came. I'll get the board."

They played two full games before conditions got so bad that they couldn't concentrate any more.

"I think the noise was the worst thing. If you could imagine having the engines of a big jet, like a 747 right outside your door — then you'd get some idea.

There was another sound that we could hear from time to time. I realised it was the vegetation being spun around in a vortex, which caused me to feel like I was caught in a giant washing machine.

Then came the calm eye of the storm, which we still found stressful, because it meant we were only halfway through the horror.

I heard some veranda roofing being ripped from the beams but figure that will be the least of our problems. What about our solar panels?

At least the house itself hasn't suffered any major damage. We managed to stay snug and safe. Thankfully the children mostly slept through the whole ordeal. We stayed with them in their room through the worst of it, just in case we had to snatch them up and move elsewhere.

When the worst was over we stumbled into bed, knowing that there would still be strong winds and a lot of rain to contend with.

I had a feeling through the worst of the storm, and it was similar to how I felt while driving through the bushfires. It is hard to explain, but... well... it was like something malevolent was trying to get at us. There were similarities in the two situations — bushfires aren't meant to occur in May, and this cyclone was unusual for this time of year, and certainly this far south. Again it felt like a battle between good and evil.

And I just realised that, when the three brothers came to do us harm, I had a similar feeling. There seems to be one guiding presence or whatever that does good, and then another force that seems intent on harm. But we've survived.

I'm rambling. It's been a big night. I'd better get some sleep now."

Although the roof of the house was covered in slippery leaves and other vegetation, her concern about the solar panels had led Meg to climb a ladder and inspect them. Luke waited below, holding the ladder and awaiting instructions.

Meg swept her gaze across the panels and found they were all still in one piece, without cracks or other damage. She crouched down and inspected the frames that held the panels in place, and they too seemed unaffected. She shook her head in disbelief and felt blessed that the people who owned the house and installed the solar energy system obviously invested heavily in the products and materials used.

From her vantage point she could see the vanes of the electricity-generating windmills. One was turning unevenly — something had bent — but she was clueless about how to fix it.

Standing in high places was something Meg enjoyed. She took a deep breath and performed a three-hundred-and-sixty degree turn. She was certain that the air quality was improving constantly, now that there were few humans to spoil it. She saw some damage in adjoining properties from the cyclone, but nothing too serious.

She had nearly completed her turn when she saw something lying on the driveway, right down near the entrance. It looked to Meg like a bundle of rags, but when she looked again, she saw skin. It was a person.

Moving gingerly to the edge of the roof, she called down to Luke. "I'm coming down — there's a person down by the road."

Finding the rungs to move backward down the ladder seemed to take ages. As soon as she hit the ground, she started running down the washed-out driveway. Rain had begun to fall heavily, and she skidded in the mud. She could see soaking wet jeans and a white shirt on a tall figure. She slid to a stop and crouched down, moving the heavy body until she could see the face. It was Derek.

CHAPTER NINETEEN

"Quick, grab him under the arms, I'll take his legs."

Transferring Derek to the house was slippery and heavy work. Twice they had to lay him back on the ground and find a better way of holding him. Meg hadn't realised how steep the driveway was until she was forced to carry a heavy load all the way to the top. The rain was streaming from the skies as though from a high-pressure hose.

As they approached the house, Meg realised the front door was closed.

"Hey Connie! Connie! Quickly, we need help. At the front door!"

They heard quick footsteps, and then the door swung inward.

"What...?"

"It's Derek. He's unconscious. Help us get him onto

my bed."

The white doona cover and sheets became smeared with mud as they lay Derek down and began stripping the wet clothes from him.

As Connie touched his skin, she flinched. "He's freezing!"

Meg put a hand to his forehead and found she was right. It was like he'd been taken from a freezer before being dumped on their driveway.

"Quickly, let's get all these clothes off. God, his boots are full of water!"

It took tremendous effort to remove first the elastic-sided boots, and then the socks that were difficult to peel from his skin. She handed them to Luke to take outside.

"Connie, we're going to have to strip him right down. You might prefer to go and turn the kettle on for the hot-water bottles."

"Yup — I'll find some more blankets as well."

Meg peeled more clothing from the freezing man and manoeuvred him and the bed-clothing until he was between sheets with the doona on top. As Luke came back into the room, she asked him to lie on top of the bed near Derek to keep him warm. She did the same from her side. As Connie began to ferry the hot-water bottles in, they placed them around him.

"Connie, can you take Luke's place? We need him outside to keep the important clean-up stuff going."

The two women lay there for another half an hour and when Maisie came to the door to see what was going on, Meg got her to lie there as well. Still the man didn't warm up.

"I don't get it, Connie. What is it? Extreme shock? Hypothermia? I've never seen anything like it."

The younger woman felt Derek's face and shook her head.

"Anyway, I have to go now and help Luke. How about I bring the kids in here and set you up with a good book? Thomas can sit on the bed, too. The two little ones — well I can put them on the floor with blankets under them. Is that okay?"

"I guess so..."

Maisie and Thomas took their duties on the bed seriously. They were unusually well-behaved, the stranger in their midst causing some concern. Strangers didn't come to their house often.

"He's been here before, kids. He was very good to you, especially you, Thomas. Whenever he held you to his chest you used to go all quiet and happy." Both children listened to Connie's words with great seriousness.

"And just think Connie, when he gets well, you'll have a paediatrician on hand. How good is that?"

By nightfall there had been no improvement in his condition. Hot soup met with unresponsive lips, and he hadn't moved from the position they had first placed him. Meg searched the pockets of his jeans for clues to where he'd been, but they yielded no clues.

She swapped positions with Connie, who needed to wash and feed the children before settling them into bed. Luke cooked spaghetti bolognese, which was eaten on trays in the bedroom. Maisie and Thomas came in for one more look before bedtime, creeping in on tip-toes and speaking in exaggerated whispers. Then they ran giggling in to bed.

When the house fell silent and Luke and Connie had gone to bed, Meg settled herself on top of the bed covers with a book. She woke after a few hours and, feeling uncomfortable in her clothes, stripped down to underwear and climbed in to bed.

She woke to movement next to her. Derek had turned on to his side and was pressing his cold body against hers. At first she thought he was seeking her warmth, but then she felt his erection against her leg. He was moving urgently and sliding around between her thighs.

Meg's body reacted instinctively and she felt herself swelling and opening. God, it had been so long! She felt him guiding himself into her from behind, and she was ready for him, but still felt a shock from his coldness in contrast to her wet warmth.

He moved urgently, holding her body tightly against his. In a couple of minutes it was over and he rolled back onto his back. He was unconscious again, or had he been all along?

Not a word had been spoken during those few, hectic minutes. She lay awake for some time, remembering how it had been between them in those weeks he had stayed with them, the easy camaraderie they shared while tackling jobs, the quiet steadiness of the man. She remembered the gentleness he displayed with Thomas, the elegance with which he would undo the tiny baby's clothing. Eventually she fell back to sleep.

She felt Derek leave the bed and moved slightly until she could watch him walk naked out of the bedroom into the living area. He was moving slowly and clumsily, not his normal graceful self. She wondered about what injuries he was carrying. Figuring he was headed to the bathroom, she wriggled back under the covers.

There was a crack of light bleeding through the curtain. It was muted, and she could hear the rain still pouring down. She thought their next job might be to build an ark and load animals on to it, two by two by two. She laughed at her own joke and thought she should tell Derek.

She was happy — aware of herself sexually for the first time in years. She had been left unsatisfied, of course, but she had a heady feeling of anticipation when thinking about how that could be remedied. She was so glad Derek was up and walking around. It spoke well of a recovery.

She strained to hear noises from the bathroom and wondered why he hadn't used the ensuite. Connie would faint if she saw him walking naked through the house. His clothes were still damp on the clothes line, though. Perhaps he'd wrap a towel around himself when he came back.

More time passed and Meg still hadn't heard any sounds. What if he'd collapsed in the bathroom? This thought made her climb quickly into her robe and head toward the bathroom.

The door was open and there was nobody inside. Meg frowned and began searching the house. One of the glass doors was slightly ajar, the rain blowing in onto the tiled floor. Just a small amount of water, which meant it hadn't been open long.

His clothes were still hanging limply on the clothesline under the verandah. The outbuildings were all shut tight.

There was a golf umbrella beside the door. Raising it she went outside, and, as she rounded the front of the house, looked in horror at the floodwaters that had appeared overnight. They were surrounded by swirling brown water — totally cut off. But where was Derek?

He was injured, naked, and sick. He had also totally disappeared.

"Gone?" Connie's mouth was open and an exaggerated frown crumpled her brow. "Gone? How do you mean..."

"Disappeared. Totally."

"So what did he tell you? What did he say?"

"Nothing. He didn't say anything."

"What, not a word?"

"Shit, Connie. That's what nothing means. Nothing!" She was almost shouting.

Connie closed her mouth — the lips spread into a thin line.

"Sorry. I'm upset. I don't understand either."

"So…what can we do?"

"Dunno. The conditions are too severe to begin searching." Meg felt tears welling. She felt Connie's hand on her arm.

"I'm the one who should be sorry. I know you wanted him to stay."

Meg turned quickly and walked out.

"How can I describe how I feel? I was so happy, so relieved he'd come back. I had something to look forward to — helping him recover and then spending time with him. It's twice as bad now — my disappointment. Worse because I just don't understand it.

This is causing such anger in me. I could have slapped Connie yesterday — slapped the young mother of four children. I'm frustrated and angry and pissed off — just so pissed off.

What would Angela do? Suddenly I don't know and what's more, I don't care.

It's not so much that I feel used and discarded — more just sad and puzzled. No, I **do** *feel used and discarded, and I reckon this is left over from what Richard and Craig did to me. The sense of abandonment and shock I felt on both those occasions still lies just under my skin. Like shingles waiting to erupt.*

The way Richard told me we were over was classic bastardry. He rang one Friday morning from work and told me to hire a babysitter.

We were going out for dinner, just the two of us. I was so excited! I didn't make the same mistake as the time we were going to the Christmas party. This time I found a sitter who could come from midday so I could spend all afternoon getting ready! I knew of a salon that did both hair and make-up and they spent hours on me. I even had a manicure and French polish. The girls in the salon advised me on the choice of an outfit, and I even purchased matching shoes and a nice necklace. I made sure Richard had no cause for complaint this time.

The strange thing was he didn't even seem to notice how good I looked. He was distracted. We went to a bistro that was upmarket — busy and noisy. He kept filling my champagne glass, almost insisting I drink quickly. Why didn't I realise what this was leading to? Because I was bloody naive, that's why. I'd spent years engrossed in my role of mother, and knew little of how things worked.

He asked how the refurbishment of my grandmother's house was going — how long before it would be liveable. I was happy he was taking an interest in it, and spent twenty minutes or so filling him in on all the details. He looked impatient and asked the same question again. I said that I'd probably put tenants in it in a few weeks and perhaps I'd start talking to rental agencies on the Monday. He said, "No, don't do that." When I asked why not, he came out with it.

He was in love with someone else. He couldn't be without her. My first question, obviously, was who? He waved his hand distractedly and said "Lucy", but gave no more details. He went on to say that he and I would divorce and he wanted the house. I could move into my grandmother's place. We would share custody of the children. He wouldn't support me — he was not required to by law — and I'd have to get a job and support myself.

He wouldn't even wait for my house to be finished. He would rent a townhouse for six weeks and put me in that. His new woman, Lucy, was to move into our family home almost immediately.

What can I say about how I felt at that time? I remember the sensation of blood draining from my head. I thought I would faint. The room darkened. A waiter came up and asked if I was all right. I just nodded. Then the tears started welling.

I remember Richard looking around the restaurant in embarrassment and suggesting I go to the bathroom to compose myself. I did this meekly, but once I was in there, and saw how good I looked, I felt stronger. I wasn't going to let him tell me what to do anymore. He'd just forfeited that right.

I went back to our table, lifted the edge of the cloth and watched all the dishes and drinks spill onto his lap. I loved seeing the range of emotions cross his face as he realised what was happening. I told him we could start the shared custody agreement that night. He could go home and look after the children because I was going out. Then I strode out of the restaurant with my head held high.

My newfound strength didn't last long. I didn't know where to go. I walked until I found an upmarket looking bar and ordered a *drink. Then another. No one approached me, or even noticed me for that matter.*

I caught a cab into the city and checked into one of the best hotels. I had nothing with me, of course; no makeup remover or hair equipment, not even any spare clothing. I drank a lot and contemplated suicide. That would teach him. Then I thought of my father and my children and how that would hurt them. The next day I went home, and moved into the rented townhouse.

You see, it wasn't so much that he no longer wanted to be with me — I can see that it was partly my fault — I'd really let myself go and didn't realise how much until I became single again. I put too much effort into raising the children — I see that now. I thought Richard was an adult who could look after himself — that he'd see how hard I was trying for the sake of our children, when really he was like a child himself, needing attention just as much as Nicky and Emily. Our sex life suffered, too, once the kids came along.

Lucy gave him what he'd been missing. As well as that, she was lithe and leggy. She had hair that was silky and flowed down to her waist. She was young, with a body not traumatised by pregnancy and birth.

No, you see — I understand how I lost him, and can sort of accept that and take my share of the blame. What I couldn't accept is the way he went about it — tossing me on the scrap-heap like that. Casting me out of the house like some broken kitchen appliance. It was done coldly, ruthlessly, and without any regard for my feelings. It was almost like he hated me.

The situation with Craig, the father of my third child, was totally different, but the sense of abandonment I felt was similar. I'd fallen pregnant accidentally. He wanted me to have an abortion. I agreed but didn't go through with it and he took this very badly. I can remember him yelling at me, red-faced and volcanic. 'I saw the signs, you know. I knew you were trying to bloody trap me, you stupid woman. All those candle-lit dinners and that lingerie — good God — didn't you know? Couldn't you see you were just a quick fuck? Did you really think that a woman like you had a chance with a man like me? You're bloody pathetic. Don't try to get any money from me, either. Don't put my name on the birth certificate or there'll be trouble. I mean that.' The door had crashed behind him as he strode out the door.

And you know, he was sort of right, too. I thought we'd make a nice couple. He wasn't much taller than me, and was stocky like me. I thought I could win him over — show him how well I could look after him. Perhaps he was right about the abortion, too. Maybe in the back of my mind I thought that if I had a child we'd end up growing closer. Pathetic when I look back now. I now know that he had 'short man syndrome' — an over-confidence in himself — thinking he was God's gift to women. Did he have to be so cruel when he dumped me, though?

Abandonment. I know what it feels like and I'm feeling it now. I'm just not sure that Derek has acted in the same way as those other two.

I don't believe he's a bastard like Richard or Craig. I don't think he just came here for sex and left again. There has to be a better explanation. The sex part seemed like an instinctive act on his part and I'm not certain he was fully conscious at the time.

Yes, the puzzle of it is like an itch that needs to be scratched. It sits on my mind and won't give me any peace.

Another day of rain has dawned and it sounds like it's still pissing down in buckets. I don't want to get out of bed — don't want to face another day of cleaning up the mess in this awful weather. I want to stay in bed and let everybody else take care of everything.

In fact, you know what? I want to move out of here. It's time I got a place of my own. It's time Luke and Connie stood on their own feet. They're old enough, mature enough. I need some Meg time, badly.

That's it. Decision made.

I'm going to start a new life.

Hey — the rain just stopped!"

The journal snapped as Meg closed it with force. Making major decisions always lifted her spirits. Now it was time to tell Luke and Connie the news.

CHAPTER TWENTY

Meg was driving the dirt roads, singing at the top of her lungs. She was house-hunting again, and this time with a relaxed anticipation. There was no hurry at all.

She chuckled to herself as she remembered Luke and Connie's faces when she told them the news. Open-mouthed shock and horror, tears, and pleading were their response.

"Guys, it's been two and a half years. Connie, I know I've been getting snappy with you. I need time to myself. I won't go straight away — we'll finish the clean-up and I'll do some other things before I go, and I still have to find a place. You'll have plenty of time to get used to the idea."

"I still need help with the babies." Her voice was a wail.

"I'll come over often to help you. I plan on living

close by. C'mon guys, it's not that bad!"

"It's Luke isn't it? It's because he doesn't hardly ever talk to you." She hit him on the leg and gave him a meaningful look.

"No, it's not that. It's sort of hard to explain." She paused and took a breath. "You know, after my marriage broke down, I had a lot of time to myself. We shared custody of the children, so I'd have long stretches of being on my own. It was the first time in my life I'd had that. I came to enjoy it. That's what I want again now."

"I sorta thought you'd help teach the kids — you know — reading and writing."

"I'd be more than happy to do that. I'll set up a school room at my place."

"How would we get them there?"

"Hmm. Why haven't the two of you learned to drive? That will be number one on the list of things to do before I go. Luke, you've been driving the tractor, so you already have an idea. We'll go and pick out a car for you — something that will hold six — and we'll make sure you know how to look after it. Hell, what the heck... we'll get two cars, one for each of you."

Luke smiled.

"Well I'm not happy about it, at all!" Connie's face

was mutinous.

"I'm not your mother. I'm not Luke's mother. I'm just someone who happened to be here when you really needed help. You're well-set-up now. You only think you need me."

Connie had stood and pushed her chair back — making it crash backward to the floor. Luke scrambled to pick it up. "Well, I'm just not happy!" She picked up her knitting and flounced out of the room, banging the bedroom door after her.

Meg slowed for a sharp corner in the road, feeling the corrugations rattling the four-wheel-drive. The roads were deteriorating with every heavy rain period, and there was no one to repair them. They were only going to get worse. She'd have to factor that into the choice of new house — make sure it was on a road that wouldn't become impassable.

Two hours a day was the time she gave herself to find the house. Two wonderful, free hours when she would drive around in high spirits — but all the time still looking out for any sign of Derek.

The gate bore a sign that read "Place of Peace and Falling Leaves", and the sign itself was of high quality, professionally painted in gold letters on a cream background.

It was so high, this property, that she could see all the way to the Glasshouse Mountains and the coast beyond. The house was constructed from rammed earth like the other, but was slightly smaller. It sat on a plateau where there was room for the large shed, pond, vegetable patch and small orchard. The front of the house was mostly glass to maximise the effect of the view.

The kitchen had marble bench tops and European appliances. The flooring was high-quality stone of some sort, rough-cut. There wasn't a low ceiling in the entire house and it felt spacious and airy.

Meg was delighted to find the bed empty. There was a vacant place in the garage where logically a car would be stored, so she supposed the owners had died elsewhere. She figured that the body disposal wouldn't have been so bad after all the time that had passed, but was still glad nonetheless.

She inspected the sturdy fence that surrounded the property with delight. This was really a stunning place and perfect for her. She felt excitement growing.

The solar panels looked as though they had withstood the cyclone but didn't appear to be generating any power. Neither were the wind turbines. She would look through the files in the study until she found some manuals about them and see why this was the case. No way was she giving this place up.

Before she left to go back to the other house, she sat on the window seat in the lounge and looked out over the pond. Birds with v-shaped wings and tails swooped down to pond level, collecting insects from the surface before rising to the calm skies. She vowed to sit here every day for at least half an hour and listen to the silence which had the effect of a tranquiliser. She was at peace.

"Shit, shit, shit. How can this be happening to me?

Another damned pregnancy test and another damned blue line. How can this be? Technically I shouldn't even have been very fertile at the time — had only finished my period a few days before — or was it? Think, Meg, think.

Well, I guess it doesn't matter now, does it? Do you know what it feels like to me? A joke. A bloody joke. Someone's playing a hell of a weird cosmic game with me and I don't like it one bit. I'm definitely not laughing.

And it's not as though it's an easy decision this time — whether to keep it or not, because it's Derek's child. Jeez. And where is he anyway? He should be here, be here for me and his child growing inside me.

*I **just don't want a baby.** It's as simple as that. It's* *dangerous for me and the child. I also just don't want one because I've just found the perfect house just for me — away from babies. Away from people who are dependent on me.*

But Derek has spent his working life taking care of babies and children. He has tended them lovingly and ensured their good health. How would it be if he returned, all fit and well again, happy to be with me — but then discover I had aborted a child — our child? How would that be?

I know what you're thinking. I could take the two pills and bring on an abortion and tell nobody. Keep it a big secret. There are two things wrong with that idea. One is that I need someone with me while the abortion is happening — Connie or Luke that is — and the other is that I am the most transparent and truthful person that ever lived, and I'd end up telling Derek. I just would. Silly, I know.

It's not like last time. This time I just can't decide."

After an absence of nearly eight months, Bill and Ben returned in the helicopter.

Meg was at Luke and Connie's, helping with the children, when they all heard the tell-tale thwock, thwock, thwock of the rotor blades. Meg jumped for the rifle while Connie herded the children into the bedroom.

The men weren't carrying a note, but had bags that looked like they contained medical equipment. Meg relaxed and put the rifle on the shelf.

The new twins were examined first, followed by Maisie and Thomas. The men performed tests and entered results into a device that looked like a tablet. With Connie they took a blood sample and gave her a bottle for urine. Luke only had to give a blood sample.

When it came Meg's turn to be examined, the man with the medical gloves, the one that had been doing all the testing, pulled her left arm out straight and she expected him to take a blood sample. His intake of breath told her he'd seen she'd removed the implant again — a fact she'd forgotten. She snatched her arm back and folded it against her other one.

The second man, the one that had been entering the data and who wasn't wearing gloves, grabbed her hand again and pulled her arm out straight. Meg stood still in shock and was barely aware of them holding the machine to her skin and implanting another device. What she'd just felt was the coldness of the man's skin — the terrible abnormal coldness that was just like Derek's. Then, as one of the men moved away with his back to her, she was reminded of the way Derek moved on the morning he left. Just like these men.

She felt faint. Sensing a chair behind her she sat suddenly and placed her head between her legs. She saw

Connie's dress approaching and a felt a hand on her back. She heard Connie telling the men that they'd done enough and should go now. They held out a bottle marked 'urine' and pointed at Meg, who blindly went to the bathroom and did what was necessary. Soon the rotors were turning and the helicopter disappeared.

Meg tried to get her thoughts in order. Facts: the weird helicopter dudes don't talk, are freezing cold, walk strangely. On his last visit, Derek didn't talk, was freezing cold, and walked strangely. Too much of a co-incidence. What the hell was going on?

"Guys, I'm stuck in a weird situation and I need to run some stuff past you."

Connie raised her eyebrows and sat down. Luke walked to the kitchen bench and leaned against it.

"I don't quite know how to start..."

One of the babies began crying. Connie sighed and pushed herself out of the seat. Luke waved her down again and brought the infant back to her.

"Just at the beginning, Meg." Connie sounded testy.

"I didn't tell you everything that happened that night when Derek was here. I felt it was personal at the time but now it's the business of all of us."

"Sounds serious."

"It is Connie. You see, I'm pregnant. It's Derek's child."

"Oh, my..."

"I didn't know what to do and kept putting off making a decision. Now I find it's too late to take the abortion pill. I really regret not taking it now."

"But..."

"Hear me out. You see...he was just like the creepy helicopter guys. I didn't realise until today."

Connie and Luke both looked at Meg with quizzical expressions.

"You don't get it. I'll explain better. Derek didn't talk the whole time he was here. He was freezing cold. When he walked out — when he left the next morning — he walked funny. I thought he was injured."

"So?"

"The guy who grabbed my arm today wasn't wearing gloves. It's the first time I've come in contact with the bare skin of either of them. His hand was like a block of ice, just like Derek's. They never speak, the same as Derek."

"But he normally does. He was just in shock or something."

"Don't you see? It's the three things."

"Meg, I think you're being a bit crazy. It was *Derek*."

"Yeah, I know it was, but he was different."

"So what are you trying to tell us?"

"I think they used Derek somehow to get me pregnant."

Connie laughed. Startled by the noise the baby detached from the breast. Luke smiled.

"Okay, I know it sounds crazy, but they've tried to get me pregnant before and failed. I reckon this was another attempt."

Connie began to look impatient. "Look, Meg..."

"No, let me finish. Think about it. I mean, who are these guys? I reckon the ones we're seeing are just a front for someone else — someone capable of manipulating our dreams, who made a paediatrician available when we needed one, who can arrange jets, helicopters, buses and hospitals as well as heart surgery. Bill and Ben aren't capable of those things. Someone is in the background, orchestrating it all. They don't want us to see them."

Connie was still looking doubtful, but Luke was nodding slowly.

"You see it don't you Luke? You don't think I'm crazy?"

He shrugged. "Maybe."

"So anyway, Meg. What are you going to do about this pregnancy?"

"I haven't got any choices anymore. It's too late to abort it using the pills. I can't think of any other way at this late stage."

"Oh, you'll have a baby too! How wonderful!" She began clapping.

Meg felt like slapping her.

Meg was overdue for a visit to the huge hardware store on the coast, so unloaded everything from the back of the four-wheel-drive and then drove it to the machinery shed to attach the trailer.

"Hey Luke. I've got my list. Do you know what you need?"

"Yup." He tapped his breast pocket and got into the passenger side.

"How about you get in this side? Practice for driving with a trailer."

He drove carefully down the rutted driveway.

"A bobcat with grader attachment. That's what we need. Fix the driveway."

"Fun!"

Meg smiled. Luke talking more was one of the nicest

things that had happened in a long time. She figured Connie had been putting some pressure on him to do so.

"It's nice having you talking, you know."

He grunted, which reminded her he could decide to regress at any time.

"No, really — it was important to me — I sorta had a sense of failure about you not talking."

"Huh? Why?"

"'Cause I felt responsible for you — caring for you. Keeping you good if you know what I mean."

"Dunno why."

"It's always been there, that feeling. Anyway — I know so much about you just by how you talk."

"Like what?"

"Private school education."

He rolled his eyes.

"Ha! I'm right, aren't I!"

"Yeah."

"You have a deep voice. Lots of testosterone. I bet you liked sports. Football?"

"Union. And Taekwondo"

"But not only sports. From some of the things you say, more so to Connie than me, I can tell you're intelligent. I think you did well in your classes. Mathematics?"

"Yup."

"Sciences?"

"Yup."

"English?" He held his hand flat and rocked it from side to side to indicate so-so.

"What did you plan to study at Uni?"

"Dunno. Sciences, I guess."

He made a turn carefully, watching the trailer in the mirrors.

"I heard you playing the guitar to Connie a few weeks ago. Nice. You sang too."

"You heard that?

"Yeah, I did. You've got a nice voice."

She was rewarded with a smile.

"But you know the best thing about having you talking, is that I've got another adult to hold conversations with. It's been pretty tough, you know.

"Yeah, I guess so."

"You're not going to stop again, are you?"

He laughed. "No."

"Promise?"

"Yeah, cross my heart."

They drove in silence for a few minutes.

"Do you know what's the most frustrating thing,

Luke — about our lives, I mean?"

"Nup."

"Before all this — back in 2013, we had such access to information. It was immediate and constant. If you take me for instance, I could access the internet on my phone, tablet and PC, and was never far from any of them. It seemed I'd only just have to reach out my hand to find a device that connected me to all the information I needed. When I became the PA of a high-profile businesswoman, I depended on this quick access to data even more." She stopped and looked at some houses that were totally overgrown with vegetation. Soon many of the man-made structures would be decomposing into the soil.

"If there was a major event happening anywhere in the world, and I'm talking war, revolution, a new virus, catastrophe of any sort, the information spread across the globe in an instant."

"Yeah, I reckon I was a bit young to appreciate it properly."

"True. But to think it was only a couple of hundred years ago that people had to wait for boats to arrive from England before they could hear news that was already six months old. For such a brief and lovely moment in time, we had the internet and the world was wide open to us."

"We could sure use it now."

"That's the thing. It's just so frustrating. I still want to check what's happening around the world, just in case there are more survivors. We just have no way of knowing. You know, something might have come up by now on why everyone died."

"You reckon?"

"No. Probably not." She chewed her bottom lip.

"But what's really bugging me now — like really bad — is that I let us come under the influence of the helicopter guys without hardly a fight, or even asking questions. You know, just because they don't talk, doesn't mean we can't ask."

"You stopped them taking us away again. That took guts."

"Yeah, but I could've done a lot more. I could have asked to see their superiors. That's it! Simple! Next time I'll ask. If they don't understand I'll give them a note."

Luke frowned. "I dunno about that. What about if they hurt Connie and the kids?"

"I don't think they're really out to hurt us at all. I think they want to keep us healthy. What I don't understand is who they are and why they're here. Also, why they impregnated me the first time, and what part they played in this pregnancy."

"I have a theory."

"Oh — good. Spill it."

"I didn't want to say it in front of Connie the other night — didn't want to scare her."

"Oh?"

"What if Derek died — in the cyclone — and they used his body somehow?"

"Gee Luke. I had sex with a dead man? Thanks a lot!"

"Sorry — but if you think about it..."

"How cold he was?"

"Yeah, and you said he was different..."

"But Bill and Ben — they're that cold. You'd think they'd be getting a bit on the nose if they'd been dead all this time."

"Chemicals pumped into their bloodstreams. Preservatives like they use on corpses."

"So...let's stay with your theory for now. How do *they* control them, whoever *they* are? I mean, to fly helicopters and jets and drive buses?"

"Dunno."

"It would be sad to think Derek died."

"Yeah."

"I liked him a lot and really hoped he'd come back and be with us."

"You or us? Which house?"

"Yours to start — you could do with his help. If things worked out for him and I perhaps that would change. If he was still alive that is — but whatever happens, I don't want another visit like last time."

"Yeah."

"Any other theories then — about who's controlling Bill and Ben?"

"Yeah — how about a group of, um, like, world leaders and famous people who knew the bad thing was coming and protected themselves. Once the threat was over, they wanted to help the world repopulate."

"Who would these people be?"

"Let's see — the US President, the guys who invented Google and Microsoft..."

"Why them?"

"Cause they'd be in a position to know something bad was on its way."

"Okay, Who else?"

"Good people — ones who have won the Nobel Peace prize — the people with power would have made sure they were protected so some good genes would be in future humans."

"Hmm. So why wouldn't these powerful and famous people want us to see them?"

"They'd just want to stay in the background. Easier that way."

"No, that doesn't work for me. I reckon if the guys who invented Google survived then they would have made sure we had internet access again really quickly."

"How long since you've tried to load any pages?"

"Ages."

"Maybe you should try again."

"I hate disappointment. Like checking lotto results and finding out you didn't win."

They drove silently for a few minutes, lost in thought.

Luke cleared his throat. "Then there's another theory."

"I have a feeling this'll be a real beaut. Shoot."

"A superior race needed to colonise urgently. Something happened where they lived. They'd had their eyes on Earth for some time..."

"Ah, alien invasion!"

"Hear me out. There are only a few who escaped and they weren't able to plan too well. They came here but carried some sort of bad disease with them. It killed most of us instantly."

"I see..."

"Or else," he was getting excited, "they figured we wouldn't let them arrive peacefully. They needed the whole planet. They killed off most of us humans but kept a few for their own purposes."

"Which are?"

"Cross-breeding, or slaves, or something. Knowledge maybe. You know, all sorts of reasons."

"Yeah, far-fetched, but I see where you're coming from."

He wriggled in his seat in excitement. "And they may be able to clone and accelerate the growth of the cloned person. Like Bill and Ben — that might be why they're so uncoordinated. They were made to grow before they were ready."

"And Derek too? That could mean that the original is still alive!" Her heart thumped at the thought.

"Yeah. Absolutely."

"Hey, they might be cloning us already. They have our DNA."

Luke frowned. "Creepy. But that would also explain why we never see them. They're aliens and they'd freak us out. They could look, like, really weird."

"Well, strangely, that theory sort of works. Alien invasion, heh?" Meg smiled at him. "Things are just so strange at the moment that we have to be thinking outside the square. Good one, Luke."

"Outside my window there are butterflies everywhere. They are mostly white, but I can see the occasional splash of blue. It's very late in the year for them to be around, but I'm glad they are.

My mind keeps returning to Luke's theories. I had already thought of variations of these theories myself, of course, but I wouldn't tell him that because he should be encouraged to use his imagination and voice opinions.

I only have one other theory — that it was just a natural disaster that killed everyone and now someone is trying to help us survivors anonymously. I don't know why...or who.

Luke also had me thinking about where Derek would live if he came back. If he was his old self of course. Would I invite him to stay in this lovely home I chose with just me in mind? Since then I've already discovered I'll be sharing with a baby, so how about a third person? Just you and me, and baby makes three? Hmm.

The sun is gently slipping away. A hush fills the atmosphere. Clouds, the colour of salmon, streak the skies. What a beautiful world this is."

CHAPTER TWENTY ONE

In Meg's dream, a large black dog had her on the ground, its face close to hers and breathing foul fumes into her face. The sharp teeth were centimetres from her throat. Another dog was behind it, making ripping and slurping noises as it feasted on her abdomen. Meg was screaming and howling in pain.

She woke, gasping for breath — the sheets saturated in sweat — and found the pain was real. Her womb was cramping. She reached for the torch on her bedside table and guided the light between her legs. No blood — yet.

She lay back on the pillows, panting. Was she miscarrying? How far along was she — seventeen weeks? Another wave of pain squeezed her until she curled into a ball.

Should she take something? What? Ibuprofen?

Paracetamol? A stiff brandy? Was there a drug to stop miscarriages?

But, wait. Did she want to stop it, if that's what it was? Only a few weeks ago she had been bemoaning the fact she hadn't taken the abortion drugs in time.

She went to the bathroom and turned on a light. Taking some toilet paper, she held it to her genitals. There were a few spots of blood — brown. What did it mean?

After filling a hot-water bottle she returned to bed and tried to soothe the cramps with heat, but it was a long and painful night.

They could tell Bill and Ben apart now. Ben had recently chipped a tooth and somehow it made Meg better able to differentiate between them.

The ultrasound machine was humming as he ran the probe around her lower abdomen, slipping it across the lubricant gel he'd applied. He looked at the images intently, and pressed buttons as shapes became visible. Meg was also watching closely, trying to make sense of what she was seeing.

The helicopter came two days after her night of cramps. It was an unusual visit — only weeks after the previous one — and Meg wondered if they knew that the pregnancy was in danger of terminating itself. How could they know that? She looked at her forearm and wondered about the implant, which she hadn't gotten around to removing.

Ben made a noise in his throat and pressed a button. Meg looked harder at the screen. He had highlighted two areas, and she looked at them, she realised with horror what she was seeing. Two foetuses. Goddamned twins! No!

She gripped Ben on his cold arm and held up two fingers with eyebrows raised. He raised two fingers in reply. No. Not possible. Not with her history of bad childbirths.

Ben finished the examination and began typing on a keyboard. A screen flashed which showed the progress of a file being transmitted. When it was finished, he motioned to Bill who began packing the equipment away.

Meg tore a page from a notebook and wrote in large, capital letters:

I WANT TO MEET YOUR SUPERIORS.

She handed it to Ben who looked at it without recognition. Obviously he had no idea what it said. "Give it to your bosses." He took the paper, folded it and placed it in his pocket.

"Can't you talk at all? Maybe you can but you've been told not to. Is that right?"

Ben frowned and then turned from her.

"Well, just make sure you pass that note on. Okay?"

The men picked up the cases and began walking comically back to the helicopter.

Connie came and stood by Meg as she watched them walk away.

"Gee, Meg. I hope you know what you're doing."

"Eh?"

"That note."

"What about it?"

"They mightn't like it. Might hurt us."

"If I thought that was a chance, I wouldn't do it. You should know that."

"How can you be so sure?"

"It's not an act of aggression — not like when I pointed a rifle at them."

"Maybe not — but still."

"Listen, I have to talk to someone about this pregnancy. I'm having twins for Christ sakes. I've had toxaemia in all three of my previous pregnancies. The last birth was a bloodbath that killed the baby. I read the chart — my own life was in danger. How in the hell can I have twins here with no medical help?" She covered her face and began sobbing.

"There, there." Connie was patting her on the arm. "It'll be okay. Yes, you're right. You need to tell someone."

The thing was — would anybody listen?

"I'm suffocating. I can't stand it anymore. The air seems thick and I can't fill my lungs properly. I keep breathing in short, shallow puffs.

I think it's some sort of panic I'm suffering. As my belly swells I'm deteriorating physically and mentally. I think I'm going mad. I have urges to grab the big, razor-sharp knife and slice my womb open and be rid of these things that are causing me so much harm.

I have dreams in which people whose opinion I respect tell me I'll be okay. My boss, Angela, and my mother both talk to me in soothing voices. I know these dreams are being sent to me by whoever orchestrates these things. I don't believe them for a moment.

I'm sick of this world. Sick of only having Luke and Connie to talk to. The days are long and seem an endless drudgery. There is no happiness and no excitement.

I just can't stand it anymore."

Bill was holding out a note:

IT IS NOT POSSIBLE FOR YOU TO MEET ANYBODY ELSE AT THIS TIME.

Meg snorted and crumpled it into a ball. "Arseholes". She kicked the paper ball to Thomas who squealed in delight and tried to kick it back.

More tests. More ultrasound images. Thirty weeks gestation and she already felt full term. She was impatient, angry, and as mad as a cut snake.

She wrote another note:

I WILL HAVE PROBLEMS DELIVERING THESE BABIES. BAD HISTORY. I WILL NEED YOUR HELP.

The note was placed in a pocket. The helicopter flew away, unsteadily as usual.

Maisie, nearly two years old, toddled up to Meg and held on to her leg. She looked up at her with a bewitching smile. Meg calmed and smiled back. She took the child's hand and led her out into the sunshine.

In the newsagent she took time to select a special notebook with high-quality paper. At home she opened it to the first page and wrote, "*My Wishes*". She turned to page three and thought for a moment before heading it, "*The Birth*".

"If there is a chance of saving the babies at the cost of my life, take it. These children will be the future of the human race and I am just someone who will become fairly useless at a fast rate. I am sick of this world, anyway."

On the next page she wrote, "*Burial*".

"I want you to bury me under the shady branches of the giant

fig. Don't worry about a coffin or any ornamentation. Just wrap me in a sheet and place a wooden marker on the grave."

The next page was headed, "*Journals*".

'Future generations will want to know what happened — what the old world was like and how it came to be the new world. I don't have all the answers, but I'm sure the contents of my journals — even just the 'log entries' of daily life, will be important to them. Please preserve the journals well. I suggest you take care to wrap them in air-tight packaging and place them in a metal container. This should be buried somewhere central in the township with a sign that says, "Time Capsule". It should also contain relics of our former lives that are now useless — mobile phones, tablets, etc. Maybe the time capsule should be buried outside the library. Yes, that's it. The library.

Connie, keep the journals going. Add to the time capsule. It's important.

"*Other Stuff*".

I'm ashamed of my recent behaviour. I haven't coped well — mentally or physically — with this pregnancy. I'm fairly certain I will not survive the birth. Don't get me wrong — I haven't given up. I will still fight to the end — but if you're reading this, then I didn't make it. Just know that I'm proud of you two. You've adapted to this world very well and without much angst. I guess it's an age thing. You don't question everything like I do. You just get on with life in this strange new world.

> *You make a perfect little family. I have grown to love you as my own. Take care now. X"*

CHAPTER TWENTY TWO

Meg was packing to move back to Luke and Connie's house when she heard the helicopter approaching. It had become a regular sound during the weekly visits by Bill and Ben, who had been conducting tests and transmitting the results to unknown recipients. This time the tone of the helicopter seemed deeper.

What she saw when she looked out the window piqued her interest. The chopper had a cable hanging from its belly and at the end of this was a large object — like a shipping container but made of a material that looked lighter.

She drove quickly to the other house to see what they'd brought. Luke and Connie were standing on the veranda, trying to control Maisie and Thomas, who wanted to run to the strange box that was being disconnected from the aircraft. The men appeared to have difficulty with this manoeuvre, and, when the box was freed, lurched crazily in the sky for several seconds before landing safely.

Everyone watched with interest as Bill and Ben ran to the box and began undoing large fasteners that held it together. The sides dropped to the ground and walls sprang up in their place. The men ran around for half an hour, assembling, propping and securing, until the structure was all in place.

From the back of the chopper they produced boxes, which they took into the small building. There were noises of packaging being undone and objects being placed.

The men worked without rest until mid-afternoon, at which time they boarded the helicopter and flew away.

They returned the next day with another container and began unpacking it very quickly. Meg took a comfortable chair and a coffee onto the veranda and spent an enjoyable time watching the activity.

Furniture was being assembled before being transferred into the building. It wasn't just normal furniture, however. It was an adjustable hospital bed, then an operating table. There was a cabinet which Meg thought might hold medicines and equipment. There were chairs and a desk.

Next came machines — lots of them.

The last object to be removed from the second

container was a generator. By nightfall it was humming, and the building was lit. At that time of evening, with the lighting glowing through the thin sides of the building, it looked almost romantic.

The next day dawned cool, wet and windy. When Meg walked into the kitchen, she saw the men standing by the glass door with a note:

PLEASE COME OVER TO THE HOSPITAL
FOR TESTS.

She nodded and closed the door quietly behind her. The wind caught her by surprise, and she quickly pulled the bathrobe up to her neck and held it closed with one hand. She crossed the damp grass as fast as her cumbersome body would allow.

As she entered the hospital she was led to a chair in the entry area. Beyond that she could see another room sealed behind clear plastic. She could see the operating table and lighting already in place.

Ben, with the chipped tooth, took a blood pressure reading. Bill drew blood from the inside of her elbow into several phials, which were taken into another room she couldn't see. Ben handed her a specimen bottle and pointed to a bathroom to the left of her chair. After she'd filled it, he took it away.

Bill came back with a note:

WE WILL OPERATE IN TWO DAYS. DO NOT
EAT AFTER MIDNIGHT ON THE NIGHT BEFORE.

Meg nodded. This was the best she could possibly
have hoped for. She only had one question — who was going
to perform the procedure?

*"I can't sleep. It's after three in the morning and I have barely
closed my eyes. Thoughts keep running through my head like bullet
trains.*

*The caesarean section will be performed today, but that's not
what's keeping me awake. I had a thought, which my over-revved brain
won't put aside.*

*You see, there is another theory that neither Luke nor I have
considered, nor do I even know how it came to be in my mind. It's rather
out there as far as theories go:*

A PARALLEL UNIVERSE.

*Do you know how much I'd give for internet connection right
now to look it up? There are some things I already know — I'd spent
time looking up the subject after reading a novel by a Japanese writer
where the protagonist finds herself in a world running parallel to her own.*

*It wasn't a new concept. Several noted physicists had supported
the idea with differing theories of how it would all work.*

One of the more prominent scientists suggested that each time there is more than one possible outcome for an action, the universe splits so that all outcomes happen, but each in a different universe. The one nearest to you could be as close as one millimetre away.

So imagine, for instance, that something truly bad was happening to someone and it looked like the outcome might be too awful for their mind to bear, it might propel them into the parallel universe where the outcome is better.

Let's apply this theory to my own situation. I was in hospital in labour. The father of this child — the photographer called Craig — was noticeably absent. I had eaten a fair-sized dinner not long before my waters broke. My specialist, who couldn't be found, had already booked me in for a caesarean on the following Friday and this was Wednesday. He had told me I should not attempt a natural birth.

The resident doctor decided to allow the labour to proceed, because it was already so advanced. He said he needed to be elsewhere but would return shortly. Everything was calm to begin with but then people were shouting and pushing buzzers. Machines were hurtling into the room. The resident came back and I could see the horror on his face. A needle was being pushed into the back of my hand and the last words I heard before losing consciousness were, "Quickly, before we lose both of them..."

What if this caused me to leap into another dimension?

I really have to run this by Luke. I'm sure he wouldn't mind me waking him."

Meg crept into Luke and Connie's room and shook Luke lightly. There wasn't any response so the shaking got rougher. "Luke...Luke..."

He opened one eye.

"I've got to talk to you. Come into the lounge."

"Whaat?"

"C'mon, it's important."

"What time is it?"

"Don't worry about that. Hey, I'll make you a hot chocolate. C'mon."

He groaned and rolled out of bed. Meg went to heat the milk up. Luke came out scratching his head.

"What's this all about?"

"We missed one idea."

"Huh? About what?"

"You know ... theories. We had natural disaster, biological warfare, aliens, and zombies. Now I've got another one."

"You woke me for this?"

"Yeah, but it's important. Hear me out. Parallel universe." She said it proudly.

Luke stared for a moment and then turned to go back into the bedroom.

"No, Luke. Stay please. Come and listen."

"Nah, this is stupid. I'm cold. Tell me tomorrow."

"Jeez, stop whining. My operation is tomorrow. Just give me five minutes, will you?"

He sat down heavily, and listened while she told him everything she knew on the subject.

"I don't get it. You get shunted into this alternate world. What about us — Connie and me. How did we get here, or were we already in this world?"

"I don't know. I'm guessing you were already here."

He looked doubtful.

"Hey, they made a movie about it once. I don't remember the name of it — I just remember a guy in a bunny suit and something about a jet engine falling on a house."

Luke stood. "No offence, Meg, but I've heard enough. Good night."

He didn't even wait for hot chocolate.

Thwock, thwock, thwock. Meg had been watering the vegetables at her own house, waiting impatiently for the helicopter to return so the operation could be performed, and now the aircraft was approaching. Once this sound had caused terror in her but now it seemed to be her only chance for survival. She turned the hose off and watched the helicopter approaching the other house, swinging from side to side like always.

She began the drive, trying to avoid any potholes or corrugations that caused discomfort to her over-stretched body. The helicopter was to her right, steadying for its descent. Then something went wrong and it began turning — the whole fuselage was spinning, and it got faster and then faster again. Meg saw it keel over to one side, but then the trees blocked her view.

She accelerated until she could see the helicopter again. It was still moving but was clearly in trouble. It hit the ground and a rotor blade was flung into the air. The cabin was breaking up. There was an explosion.

Meg drove to the other house, sounding the horn as she drove up the driveway. Luke was already outside, looking in the direction of the crash.

"Jump in. We'll go and see if we can help."

Another explosion rent the air. Meg drove quickly, arriving within minutes.

Parts of the helicopter were strewn over a large area. There were fires. Meg pulled over and Luke ran toward the wreckage. She grabbed the first-aid kit and followed him as quickly as she could.

As she reached his side, Luke shook his head. "No one could live through this."

The fire in the cabin was burning with the heat of a furnace. Meg and Luke stood and watched helplessly until the flames died down and they could see the charred remains of three figures that were strapped in the smoking seats. *Three.* One would have been Bill or Ben, piloting the craft. Of the other two, one might or might not have been the other of Bill or Ben. There would have been either one or two other people being transferred to the hospital.

The full horror of what this meant hit Meg.

"Luke — who's going to perform the operation now?" As she watched the blood drain from his face she knew that any hope of a trouble-free birth had just gone up in flames.

Connie's eyes were huge.

"So what are you going to do now?"

"Dunno, Connie. How are you with a scalpel?" She shuddered, and Meg turned to Luke.

"How about you? Do you have a steady hand?" He backed away, waving hands in a blocking gesture.

"Derek would have been able to help, somehow. But then there's the anaesthetic as well. Someone has to administer that."

They all fell silent.

"Do you know what really pisses me off? The other or others in the chopper. We almost got to meet them — might have solved a part of the mystery."

"They'd probably have stayed out of sight, though."

"Possibly, Luke — but let me tell you something, I would have found a way to see them!"

He smiled and nodded.

"Okay — so we have to think calmly and rationally. I have to have these babies before my condition worsens. Bill and Ben knew that from the tests they were performing, which was why they were going to operate today."

"I sorta don't understand what might happen if you try to have them naturally. You've never really explained..."

"There are two main problems. I've had three caesareans, and it's considered a risk to have a natural birth after them. Risk of rupture — that sort of thing. Then I'm prone to pre-eclampsia. I've had it for all three pregnancies and it's really unpredictable. If it turns into full-blown eclampsia, well, that's just catastrophic to me as well as the babies. Organ damage, seizures, death."

"Oh, I see."

Meg bit her lip and thought. No ideas came to mind.

She was starving — had been fasting since midnight. "No chance of a sandwich huh, Connie?" The younger woman moved into the kitchen and opened the refrigerator. Her voice came from its depths.

"Induce the births?"

Meg sat straighter. Yes, that might be a chance.

"Any idea how, Connie?"

"No, but I read about it once in those books you got on giving birth."

Meg went to the bookshelf and ran her hand along the titles. "Here we go." She checked the index and found the page. Connie brought her food, but she ate unconsciously, totally absorbed in the contents of the text book. From time to time she would move position in an attempt to ease the weight of the unborn children.

"Luke — come with me, please? We need to find some hormone gel."

Connie came out from the kitchen. "How does it work?"

"Hopefully it works really well. I haven't got time for explanation, sorry. Later. Let's go." She threw the keys to Luke. "You drive."

The birthing unit of Nambour General Hospital sat to one

side of the main building and to Meg it seemed as insurmountable as Mt Everest.

"We might just sit for a few minutes — sorry. I've gone all weak and floppy. Must've been rushing to the crash this morning."

Luke pushed his seat back and closed his eyes. "No probs. Just nudge me."

Silence fell in the car.

"The guys were really bad chopper pilots weren't they?"

Luke pulled his cap over his eyes. "Hmm."

"They were always flying as though they couldn't gain proper control. I guess it might have been to do with their total lack of co-ordination."

"Could be."

"Do you still think the other one or two in the cabin could have been aliens?"

"Yup."

"We got so close..."

"Yup."

"Hey Luke, I don't reckon I can go in. I've just sorta fallen in a heap."

He pushed his cap back.

"Ah, okay. What are we looking for?"

Meg looked at the paper. "It's Dinoprostone gel — a prostaglandin. There are a few different brands so it might be hard to track down. Here, take the paper."

He looked at it and mouthed the syllables.

"Look at the use by dates too. If they've all expired, take the most recent. Bring a few different ones."

"Can you use anything else— other than this?"

"Just Misoprostol which is another prostaglandin. That's in tablet form. I think the gel might be more effective.

"Ah, okay."

"You know what Luke — I'm just flying by the seat of my pants. I don't know what I'm doing. This could go really bad."

"Or good."

Meg laughed. "True. I'm a bit scared though."

In a rare show of affection, Luke leaned over and hugged her. It brought tears to her eyes.

Luke jumped out of the car and ran into the Birthing Centre.

Meg was startled awake by the sound of the car door opening. From the lengthening shadows, she could tell Luke had been gone for considerable time.

He passed a large bag to her. Inside were around ten boxes of various shapes and sizes. He leaned over and removed a flat, rectangular package. "This one's the best."

She unfolded the instructions and began reading them. They were the same as what she'd read in the books. Luke started the car.

"Wait a sec. I need apply this right now. I'll do it in the back seat. Look away."

It was awkward — the application — and messy. Meg asked Luke to get tissues from the glove box and pass them over.

"Okay, I have to lie still for at least thirty minutes, which is how long it'll take us to drive home anyway. I'll stay in the back here — avoid potholes and speed bumps, please."

"I slept a lot today. I've got no hope of falling asleep quickly. The house is quiet.

I've left my curtains open and can see the hospital waiting there for me. A hospital with no doctors or other medical staff. I took a look around there before bedtime — went from tiny room to room, looking at instruments in sterile packages that were lined up in rows.

I think I want the birth to happen in this bed, my favourite one. Three and a half years ago I loaded this ensemble into the back of a removal van and brought it here. Connie didn't touch this room after I

moved to my new place — it's still completely mine. So I won't go over to
the hospital. Whatever happens will happen here where I'm most
comfortable.

I'm not feeling wonderful. These babies can't come quickly
enough."

The contractions began at four in the morning. Initially, Meg
didn't feel the need to wake Connie; she thought there was no
rush. Within fifteen minutes, however, the pains came faster
and faster.

"Connie! Connie!"

The younger woman came in to find Meg writhing in
pain. "There, there. This is good. Just what we wanted. Hold
my hand."

The contraction eased and Connie put a cool hand
washer to Meg's forehead.

"I've been knitting for your babies, you know."

Meg was panting, her eyes half closed.

"What colour?"

"Some pink, some blue."

"A boy and a girl?"

"Yes, I think so."

"Why?"

"Well, it's complicated, but you see — I think there's a plan for us to start repopulating the world as quickly as possible. That's why there are all these twins. We need a male to impregnate our girls and we also need a female for Thomas to mate with. That way we get the most from this tiny gene pool."

Even through her pain and growing weakness, Meg was surprised. This was a high level of thought for the young woman.

"Connie...the book...on the table there."

"This notebook?"

"Yeah, see the first page — about the births?"

Connie's eyes grew wide as they skimmed across the words.

"Oh, no Meg! No!"

"Yes, absolutely. That's what I want. Save the babies in any way you can."

"Silly, Meg. It won't come to that. Soon you'll give birth and everything will be fine."

Another huge contraction. Meg felt something shifting in her brain.

"C'mon Meg. I've been through this. I know what it's like — what works. Breathe through the pain..."

Another lull.

"The end of the story..."

"What's that Meg? Speak up."

"If I wrote this story, the story of us here, of all that had happened — the end..." She was whispering.

Connie leaned closer to hear. "Yes, Meg? What about the end?"

"The last scene would be all of us sitting at the big table on the front veranda. The one we've never used much. We'd be sitting there having a cool drink on a hot afternoon. All icy..."

"The drinks are all icy. Okay. What next?"

"We'd hear voices. Loud, happy voices. We'd look at each other in wonderment and stand to see where they were coming from."

"And?"

Meg was hallucinating, whispering softly. "They would come walking up the driveway — a whole lot of them and Derek would be leading them — lovely Derek, and there would be around six other adults and an assortment of children, all twins. The future of the human race would be walking up our driveway, led by Derek... and he would look at me with love in his eyes..."

Meg saw a flash of light but it came from inside her own head and then there was a bolt of pain that shot through her brain. Connie was screaming out for Luke as Meg's world went black.

CHAPTER TWENTY THREE

Meg wakes slowly, trying to focus her eyes. She coughs; her throat feels terrible. It is raw and sore, and her whole body feels like she's been hit by a truck.

There are shapes by the bed, and as they become clearer she can make out a strange sight. It is Richard —her ex-husband — and he is holding a wrapped bundle. It looks like a baby, but how could it be? He's smiling — Richard is — and his whole face wears an expression of pride and concern. His eyes shine with the sort of love she has never seen in them before.

"Hello, my brave darling girl. Don't try to talk, will you?"

Meg shakes her head.

A nurse sails in — the old type with a big bust and

bossy attitude. "Ah, that's a sight for sore eyes, that is. She's awake. Don't try to talk, dear. I'm going to find Doctor."

Meg points to her throat and raises her brows. "Oh, they had to insert a tube into your airway. It was done in a hurry — they might have done a bit of damage."

She wants to ask hundreds of questions. Why is she here? More to the point, why is *he* here?

"I nearly lost both of you. It was touch and go. They got this little one out first and then concentrated on saving you. I knew you'd want it that way."

Oh you did, did you?

"You were in a really bad way. They felt the best option was to induce a coma. The problem was they couldn't bring you back. Scary times."

Whoa.

"You were like that for days. Then you began to come around this morning. They called me and I got here as quickly as I could."

And where are Nicholas and Emily?

"I was really scared you know. I thought it was all over." His eyes are welling. Richard crying? Weird.

"But we're all here safe and sound now. You and I, and our firstborn — a boy."

Firstborn?

"It looks like he'll be an only child. Lots of damage to you, poor darling. The doctor will tell you about that later."

As if on cue, the nurse sails back in alongside a young doctor.

"Ah, excellent. Sleeping beauty has awoken. I'm not your usual attending — Doctor Forbes isn't here right now — but we'll let him know you're back with us. He'll drop in soon."

He feels her pulse and gazes at various machines. Then he scribbles on her chart for several minutes.

"Your blood pressure has normalised which is great news. We're going to start reducing some of the drug dosages and monitor the results. We'll also get an ENT man to come and look at your throat. Damage under these circumstances is common."

He keeps scratching at the chart. "Now, Richard. Have you filled Meg in on what happened?"

"Haven't really had time yet. Just basics."

"Okay, well Doctor Forbes will want to tell her the details anyway."

"What about brain activity?"

"Absolutely. We'll run another test. She looks good, though." He raises his eyes to hers. "Richard is asking about brain activity because, while you were in the coma, you scared us a bit. There wasn't much going on. We'll run another test now you're awake."

Meg is trying to absorb all of this.

"Don't be alarmed. It was probably just a glitch. I reckon we'll soon have you unhooked from all the machines and you'll go home with your new baby."

Richard looks pleased. He rocks the bundle with more energy.

"Have you named him yet?"

"Nah, been waiting for Meg. We've picked out three names and were just waiting to see what he looked like."

Meg motions to the doctor for his pen. He passes that and his little spiral notebook to her. She writes "*Derek*" in big letters.

Richard stops rocking the baby. "Derek? We didn't pick that one!"

Meg stabs the paper and looks at him with thin lips.

"Okay, okay. Derek it is. I guess you've earned the right to name him. But where did it come from?"

She leans back on the pillow and closes her eyes. The nurse clicks her tongue and adjusts the bedclothes. "Time to leave the poor lass in peace. Off you go now. You can come back later."

Meg sleeps the sleep of the dead for the next twelve hours. She wakes feeling fresher, uncurls and stretches. Then, noticing Doctor Forbes hovering in the doorway, she smiles and motions him in.

He talks for ages, telling her the story of a birth that just kept going wrong. "I was at another hospital attending a birth. When I finished, there was another just down the hallway. I was on the phone constantly to the people here, giving them instructions about how to proceed, but the situation rapidly worsened."

He removes his glasses and massages the bridge of his nose. "It was just one situation presenting itself after another. I won't go into details now, that'll keep for another time — but we ended up deciding to induce a coma in an effort to try and stabilise you. That helped, but then you went too deep. It seemed that you just didn't want to come out of it again."

She nods to show she is following him.

"Your brain activity was abnormally low, but has come back to normal now. We were very pleased to see that." He pulls a tiny torch from his pocket and flashes light into one eye and then the other.

"I must say your recovery is brilliant now. The drug dosages have been reduced without problems. You'll be home in no time."

Meg smiles but doesn't feel happy. She has to go home to Richard? Then there's the little stranger — a baby she's never known — hasn't even felt in her womb.

"The ENT man said the tissues of your throat are still too swollen to determine the full extent of the damage. He'll look again in a couple of days. He asked that you don't talk until then."

She nods. Not talking was proving to be a godsend. No wonder Luke indulged in it for so long.

"Richard said he'd told you there was a lot of internal damage. Here's the bad news. We had to remove your uterus. Sorry."

Meg feels that this is the least of her problems. She is still just trying to work out her place in the strange new world she has found herself in. Doctor Forbes is watching her closely, waiting for her reaction to the news about her uterus. She shrugs and smiles. Easy come, easy go.

"Okay, well I think that's about all I need to trouble you with today. A physio will come by later to put you through some light exercises. Richard's waiting outside — so I'll choof off and come back tomorrow."

She gives the thumbs up sign.

"Here you go, Richard. She's all yours. Don't stay too

long."

The doctor makes some notes on the chart and waves as he leaves.

"The baby is still asleep. Thought I'd leave him that way. How are you today?"

She nods.

"Great. Hey, are you sure about that name — Derek?"

She frowns and crosses her arms.

"Okay, okay. I just thought you might have been, I dunno, a bit woozy yesterday. Made a mistake or something."

She shakes her head.

"Fine — whatever you want. Now, what do you need me to get for you? Your wish is my command."

Meg motions for a pen. Richard goes to the nurses' station and returns with a sheet of A4 paper and a blue ball point pen. Meg frowns at the pen — a horrible cheap thing — but begins to write. She starts with the word "*List*" at the top of the page.

"This looks ominous."

She smiles and the pen begins to move down the page, each item numbered:

1. *Journal with good quality paper — French*
2. *Fountain pen, good brand, 3 boxes of refills*

3.   *Ordinary notebook for communicating with people*

4.   *Felt tipped pen for   3*

5.   *My tablet— it will need a mobile broadband SD card from the Telco*

6.   *Mobile phone*

7.   *A photo from our wedding*

Richard's face brightens when he sees the last item. "Aw, that's nice. I'll bring one in a nice frame." Meg smiles, but falsely. She doesn't want the photo for any romantic reason — more to check on how it differs from the one she remembers.

Richard points to number five, frowning. "Tablet? You don't have one. I can buy you one if you really need it." He sounds like it is the last thing he wants to do.

Obviously her very expensive state-of-the-art tablet no longer exists, or never did. This is going to be hard, working everything out. She points to number five and adds, 'a good one'.

"Well, okay — I suppose. You've come out of that coma with expensive taste. I'll get all this for you." His voice sounds resigned.

Do they have money problems? They never used to. Bummer!

Richard stays for a few more minutes, conducting the one-sided conversations. Meg pretends to doze off so he'll go. She needs the stuff on the list.

He bends and kisses her on the cheek. "I'll be back later, with some of this stuff. I may not be able to get all of it. I'll bring the rest tomorrow."

She frowns and shakes her head. She makes a big shape with her hands.

"All of it. You want all of it today? Wow. Okay then. I'd better get moving. Hey, when you want to see...um...Derek, just ask the nurse. Bye, darling."

At last she is alone with her thoughts. She has to get things right in her brain.

Meg smiles as the web browser loads. Internet at last. She has so many things to look up she doesn't know where to start. The date. There it is. The thirteenth of July, 2013. That doesn't fit in with the date when everyone died, or the last date she knew in Maleny, which was August 20th, 2016. This is like some date plucked from a calendar by a mischievous child.

Next she visits the website of the merchant bank Richard works for. His profile isn't among the management team. It isn't there at all. She does a web search for Richard Atkins and there are absolutely no results. He's obviously not a high-flier anymore. Maybe he never has been one.

That means he would never have been working with Lucy — the one that caused the end of their marriage. Interesting.

Nicholas and Emily seem to have never existed. She wonders about her parents. Are they alive?

So where are she and Richard living now? She does a search of the white pages, but there are no entries. They have always had a silent number, though.

Another big breasted old nurse barges into the room, and makes tut-tutting noises. It is late. She takes the tablet from Meg and puts it in a drawer. Pills are handed to her in a cup, and Meg swallows them.

She tries to make more sense of everything, but falls into a confused sleep.

"So this is my new journal. I hope it's as good as the old ones for working on problems, because I have a few.

I'm back in my old life but it's different. In weird ways. Richard is my husband and he's nice. Likable, but you know, the old wounds are still too fresh. He's so nice he seems a bit sinister — like a shark in a dolphin suit.

I have a son whom I don't feel any attachment toward. I guess that will improve with time.

The other thing is colour. This will sound really strange, but where I am now — this world— has less colour than the one I was in — the Maleny one, I mean. The other one was just so vivid, so alive, and so damned colourful. This one is muted and washed out.

I'm confused and scared. I don't know who to turn to. I don't know what's real any more. I need help.

Perhaps I can ask the doctor some questions tomorrow. That might be a good idea."

"Hi Meg. How are you feeling today? Oh, a note! Great."

Dr Forbes reads it and frowns.

"Oh yes. I know of several cases where patients have had very realistic dreams when in ICU. There's actually a name for it — ICU psychosis. I had a woman patient who came out of critical care convinced she'd been on a cruise with friends for the entire time. She told me about the meals they had eaten and the European ports they'd called in to. She'd even ridden a donkey up a hill in Greece." He laughs.

"They think it's caused by a combination of things: morphine and other drugs, the state of the brain." He stops suddenly and looks at her closely. "Been for a wee holiday yourself then? I can get someone more expert to talk to you about it."

She shakes her head, and acts with nonchalance.

"Ah okay. Well, anyway — good news. Home in two days. I've told Richard and he'll bring you clothes and get a baby seat installed in the car." He takes her hand. "You've come through this very well. You'll just need further treatment on that throat and then you'll be one-hundred-percent."

"One hundred percent? I don't think so. My uterus is missing for a start. Ninety-seven percent?

Had I woken with a voice that worked, I believe I would have been labelled as suffering with ICU psychosis. Can you imagine the questions I would have asked within minutes of waking? Where are Nicholas and Emily? Richard, you bastard, what are you doing here? Why aren't you off screwing that Lucy woman? Why isn't everyone in the world dead except me and a handful of others? Ha!

I don't think I'm suffering from any psychosis. I feel very sane. I think that the first terrible labour tipped me into the parallel universe where Luke, Connie and I lived. Then the next labour pushed me into this one, which is similar to the first, but different.

How will I ever know for certain? It seems important to me that I find out. Actually it seems vital to my sanity.

I've thought out a plan. I'll tell Richard to bring my clothes tomorrow, along with my handbag and purse and things. He'll question it, but the new Richard is a hell of a lot more compliant than the old one. I'll give him a reason why I want them a day early and he will swallow it.

I know the rhythms of the hospital now. When it's quiet I'll get dressed and slip out.

There should be cabs waiting outside. I'll get one to take me to the closest car rental agency. A small, sporty number I think. I'll be doing a lot of kilometres.

I'll drive to Maleny like I did before. I'm in a similar condition to when I did it the first time so will know how to pace myself. If I find the house — the lovely first rammed earth one I lived in, surely that's proof? Then I'll look for the second one. Double proof. Is it? Maybe I've already seen them in this life I'm in now. Maybe it's not one-hundred-percent sure.

I've looked up paediatricians in Sydney and there's one called Derek. His home address is in Coogee. If I get a look at Derek and he's the same as the one in Maleny, is this absolute proof?

Or the time capsule. I could go to the library and see if one has been buried there. Would it be there yet? How does this time thing work? I'm getting confused.

So I'll go and do these things. If I find none of them — what does that mean? Perhaps it means I should return here for treatment.

Or maybe not.

Wish me luck."

Dear Reader,

The sequel to this story, "In a Time Where They Belong" is now available through Amazon (print and Kindle editions), as well as the other usual outlets.

If you would like to be advised when future publications by Brenda Cheers become available, simply email:

birdcallpublishing@gmail.com

The *'Brenda Cheers – Author'* Facebook page will also provide this information. *'LIKE'* the page to receive updates.

We hope you enjoyed this story. Reviews and ratings on Amazon are always greatly appreciated.

Thank you.

Birdcall Publishing

ACKNOWLEDGEMENTS

This novel wouldn't have made it to print if it wasn't for those wonderful people who selflessly give their time when requested. They are the beta-readers who check drafts and offer constructive criticism. Terry, Robyn, Rebecca, Jessica and Lee - thank you.

I need to offer special thanks to Tracey who has become the guardian angel of my manuscripts. I can't tell you how much this means to me.

ABOUT THE AUTHOR

Brenda Cheers is a writer of both short and long fiction.

She lives in Brisbane, Australia with her partner and two daughters.

See more at www.brendacheersbooks.com

www.ingramcontent.com/pod-product-compliance
Lightning Source LLC
Chambersburg PA
CBHW050925030726
47503CB00007BB/2477